4/a

D0407275

Purchased from
Multnomah County Library
Title Wave Used Bookstore
216 NE Knott St, Portland, OR
503-988-5021

BEING
TOFFEE

Also by Sarah Crossan

The Weight of Water
Apple and Rain
Moonrise

With Brian Conaghan
We Come Apart

BEING
TOFFEE

SARAH CROSSAN

BLOOMSBURY

NEW YORK   LONDON   OXFORD   NEW DELHI   SYDNEY

BLOOMSBURY YA
Bloomsbury Publishing Inc., part of Bloomsbury Publishing Plc
1385 Broadway, New York, NY 10018

BLOOMSBURY and the Diana logo are trademarks of Bloomsbury Publishing Plc

First published in Great Britain in May 2019 by Bloomsbury Publishing Plc
Published in the United States of America in July 2020 by Bloomsbury YA

Text copyright © 2019 by Sarah Crossan

All rights reserved. No part of this publication may be reproduced or transmitted in any form or
by any means, electronic or mechanical, including photocopying, recording, or any information
storage or retrieval system, without prior permission in writing from the publisher.

Bloomsbury books may be purchased for business or promotional use. For information
on bulk purchases please contact Macmillan Corporate and Premium Sales Department at
specialmarkets@macmillan.com

Library of Congress Cataloging-in-Publication Data
Names: Crossan, Sarah, author.
Title: Being Toffee / by Sarah Crossan.
Description: New York : Bloomsbury Children's Books, 2020.
Summary: Allison runs away and, in what she thinks is an abandoned house, finds a home with
Marla, an elderly woman with dementia who believes her to be an old friend named Toffee.
Identifiers: LCCN 2020014880 (print) • LCCN 2020014881 (e-book)
ISBN 978-1-5476-0329-9 (hardcover) • ISBN 978-1-5476-0327-5 (e-book)
Subjects: CYAC: Novels in verse. | Identity—Fiction. | Runaways—Fiction. | Dementia—Fiction. |
Old age—Fiction. | Child abuse—Fiction.
Classification: LCC PZ7.5.C76 Bei 2020 (print) | LCC PZ7.5.C76 (e-book) | DDC [Fic]—dc23
LC record available at https://lccn.loc.gov/2020014880

Typeset by RefineCatch Limited, Bungay, Suffolk
Printed and bound in the U.S.A. by Berryville Graphics Inc., Berryville, Virginia
2 4 6 8 10 9 7 5 3 1

All papers used by Bloomsbury Publishing Plc are natural, recyclable products made
from wood grown in well-managed forests. The manufacturing processes conform to
the environmental regulations of the country of origin.

To find out more about our authors and books visit www.bloomsbury.com
and sign up for our newsletters.

For Aoife

They may forget what you said—
but they will never forget
how you made them feel.
—Carl W. Buehner

BEING
TOFFEE

Her Name Is Marla

Her name is Marla,
and to her I am Toffee,
though my parents named me Allison.

    Actually
it was Mum who made that decision;
Dad didn't care about a bawling baby
and her name
the day I showed up.

        He had more important things on his mind.

And now,
Marla sleeps in a bedroom next to mine
with forget-me-nots
        climbing the papered walls,
snoring,
        lying on her back, lips
                                    parted.

Sometimes, at night,
she wakes,
wails,

flails, and begs the air to
　　leave her alone, leave her alone.
　　I scuttle in,
　　stroke her arm with my fingertips.
　　I'm here. It's okay.
　　You're just having a bad dream.

That usually settles her:
she'll look up
　　like I'm the very person she expected to see,
　　shut her eyes and
　　float away again.

The mattress on my bed is so soft I sink.
The cotton sheets are paper-thin
　　from too much washing.
Nets, not curtains, cover my window:
　　streetlights blare in.

　　This is not my home.
　　This is not my room.
　　This is not my bed.

　　I am not who I say I am.
　　Marla isn't who she thinks she is.

I am a girl trying to forget.
Marla is a woman trying to remember.

Sometimes I am sad.
Sometimes she is angry.

And yet.

Here,
in this house,
                    I am so much happier
                    than I have ever been.

At the Bus Station

A bearded man sits
    by me on the bench
    in the bus station.
His nails are broken, dirty.
    His sneakers have holes in the toes.
Want a Pringle?
He conjures a red tube from his khaki coat.
    I edge away,
    focus on the backpack by my feet
    stuffed with clothes, bread rolls.
I couldn't carry much—
didn't have much to take anyway.

What the hell happened to your face?
The man squints, crunches on the Pringles,
    slides toward me.
There are crumbs on his coat,
in his beard.
Looks like someone got you good.

I turn away
hoping
    he'll think I don't understand,
    mistake me for a foreigner.

And I feel it today,
an alien far from home already,
the world all noise and nonsense.

A bus pulls up. I hand the driver my ticket,
    a yellow square to Elsewhere
    paid for with Dad's card.

            Runaway.
            Liar.
            Thief.

In a seat near the back
I press my forehead against the
cold, sweating window.

I am heading west—
    to Kelly-Anne,
    who never wanted to go—
    never wanted to go without *me* anyway.

The bus revs and shudders.

I am leaving.

The Ruby Ring

Her suitcase bulged in the middle
like it had overeaten.
She must have packed the day before—planned it.
Sorry, Allie, I gotta get out.
He's getting worse.
Kelly-Anne took off the dull ruby ring Dad had
given her.

Her face was bloated and pale.
No smile in weeks.

Still.

Don't go.
I yanked at her jacket.

Come with me.
      Her eyes were on the wall clock,
      feet in her boots.
We'll get somewhere cheap and
work it out, yeah?
Go and throw some stuff into a bag.
Do it quickly.
Come on. Quick!

I let go.
Don't you love him?

He's a bastard, Allie.
She had a plummy bruise on her arm to prove it.

Don't you love me?

I can't stay. And I can't explain.
She eyed the ring.
Surely you above all people can understand.

I do but . . .
My forehead felt hot.
My knees locked.
He isn't all bad, is he?
He works so hard.
He's tired.

Allie—

We could make him happier together.
Both of us.
We could try again.

I can't try anymore, she snapped.
She twisted my wrist.
She'd never
hurt me before,
yet here she was
stacking it up.
You don't need to stay here.
She unintentionally gestured to the mirror—
to herself.
The reflection stared back,
broken and
unconvinced.

What she didn't realize was that
I didn't have any choice.
I had to stay.
       He was my dad, not my boyfriend.
       You can't just walk out on your parents.
Who else did I have apart from him?
Who did he have but me?

I sobbed in the hallway.
Kelly-Anne pulled a scrunched-up ten from her
bag,
a coin hidden inside like a present.

Here, she said,
as though money might make it all right.
I'll get settled and call you.
Be strong and don't piss him off.
Tell him you didn't see me leave.
Make him believe I'll be back
so he doesn't look for me.

And that was that.

I watched her from the window,
worrying about what would happen when
Dad got home
and discovered his fiancée was gone,
      the engagement ring left on the hall table,
      the same red ruby that had belonged to my
      mum
      back when he loved her
      best.

The M5 Motorway

This road must be the longest in the universe.
      Concrete and concrete and concrete.

I fiddle with my phone,
      follow the jagged blue line to Bude.

A few months ago I would have spent the journey
sending Jacq crude emojis
and taking sly photos
of losers on the bus,
      their mouths gaping open in sleep.

      Now I have no one to message
      and nothing to go back to.

      I hope Kelly-Anne still has space for me
      in her life.

Concrete and concrete and concrete.
The longest road in the universe.

Bude

Buckets and spades
        hang from an awning.
Titan-white gulls yap overhead.
A gaggle of girls slurp ice cream from waffle cones
despite a slight drizzle.
        One girl pauses
then suddenly skips after the others:
        Wait up!

I lug my bag after me
                        down the
                                    steps of the bus
and on the pavement,
inhale salty air.

I have an address on a scrap of paper,
a map on my phone.

It is two miles to Kelly-Anne's place.

Forever

A man in a checkered soccer shirt
opens the door. *Yeah?*
He unashamedly stares at my cheek.

Is Kelly-Anne home?
My shoulders are burning.
I put down my backpack.

Kels? Nah.
I doubt we'll see her again.
She buggered off, didn't she?
He lifts junk mail from the mat,
flicks through it,
    steps outside
    and bungs it into a recycling bin.
She's in Aberdeen.
Got a job in sales. Owes me rent.
He picks his ear, stares at his finger
like he might discover something fascinating.
Try her phone. Not that she'll answer.

I'll try.
    I don't tell him
she hasn't replied to my messages recently either,

or that it seems pointless
if she's in Aberdeen and
I've come to Cornwall.

We are a whole country apart.

You all right?
The man examines my backpack.

I better go, I say.

Do you have somewhere to go?
His expression has softened.
A cat is nudging his sneakers.

I don't know.
But not home,
I know that for sure.

The Mark

I tap
my cheek
with the tips
of my fingers.

It is still hot.

Shed

The air is bruised by the blast of fireworks
and the dusk smells faintly of gunpowder
though it's weeks until Guy Fawkes Day.

Straight ahead
        a gravelly lane separates
two rows of gardens,
and despite Google Maps telling me to
        turn right,
I cut through it, back into town,
down toward the sea.

In one garden,
        a greenhouse with moldy windows.
In another,
        a collection of toys piled into a pyramid.
In the next,
        a stack of deck chairs and folding tables.

But near the end of the lane
        is a ramshackle shed,
        its door ajar,

overshadowed by an abandoned house—
no lights on inside,
ivy like lace across its windows.

I slip through a gap in the fencing,
push open the door to the shed,
        slip inside.

It is strewn with rusting cans of paint,
        a split bag of cement.
Heavy tools hang from hooks;
the one small window looking onto the lane
is curtained over with a torn cardigan.

I can use my sweater as a pillow.
I can lie with my feet against the door.

    There are worse harbors.

Nothing

I check my phone
though I haven't switched off the sound,
would easily have heard a ping,
but still nothing from Kelly-Anne.

And nothing from Dad either.

I try lying down,
imagining tomorrow's sun
and pleading with sleep to swallow me
before the night rushes in with full force
and switches on the fear—
                not of rats or mice
that might, in the night,
nibble away at my burn
like it's barbecued meat,
tender and theirs for the taking,
                but of people
and how they could hurt
an already damaged girl
                    hunkering
                    alone
                    in the dark.

I reach for a rusty wrench,
feel its weight in my hand,
then
        swing with all my might
at an invisible stranger,
at looming danger.

        My face stings.

I drop the wrench and close my eyes.

My phone remains silent.

During the Night

Shuffling, scuffling noises outside the shed
like boots on gravel.
I sit up, surprised I've slept.

The door creaks,
I squeak,
and slinking into the shed
like silk
comes a gray cat
with luminous mini-moon eyes.

Pss-pss-pss-pss-pss, I hiss,
tapping my fingertips together,
offering an empty hand.

The cat noses the air,
then turns,
tail aloft,
ass exposed,
shunning my affection.

Popcorn

He suggested a
Movie Night,
said we'd watch anything I wanted
    after he'd had a
    quick shower.
He loved
    The Full Monty,
it made him laugh out loud,
so that was what I chose,
    what I wanted for us both,
    had the TV ready and everything.

He also liked salty popcorn,
fresh,
so I made some
in a pan on the stove,
the corn
       pop
           pop
               popping into puffs.

But I popped so much
the oil got too hot,
the kitchen too smoky,

and the alarm was raging,
filling the house with
noise.

Dad ran into the kitchen, hair wet.
Jesus hell! he shouted,
and before I could
explain about his
                popcorn
                surprise
he had me by the wrist
and was twisting it,
twisting it,
and hurting me into the yard,
where I was made to
sit
for several
cold hours
and think carefully
about my behavior.

Bruised

I cannot get back to sleep,
so I pull a banana from my bag
and peel it.

> Brown spots
> dot its length.

> I throw it aside.

> I have never
> been able to eat
> bruised fruit.

Cover Up

There wasn't much I couldn't hide
with sleeves, a pair of tights,
and a forged note from home:
Allison can't do PE today
        because blah blah blah.

The teachers rolled their eyes
(unsympathetic to period pain)
and let me sit on the sidelines.
My classmates trampolined in their shorts and T-shirts,
        front-dropping,
                        somersaulting,
                        soaring
                        into the ceiling of the gym,
howling from the fun of it,
                        the freedom,
while I had time to plot
how to stay out of Dad's way
that day
and give the blue bruises a chance
to fade to yellow.

Breakfast on the Beach

Waves steamroll the sand
while toddlers eat fistfuls of it.
I buy a bag of open fries
with my last bit of cash,
      Dad's card declined already,
and drown them in vinegar,
finish them off with a pink lollipop
like I am eight years old.

Then the sky starts to spit,
dotting the sand into darkness,
and I've got nowhere to hide but back in the shed.

      So that is where I head.

The Empty House

The wide windows are shut tight
but much cleaner up close than they seem from the
                                                    end
                                        of the garden.

With cupped hands against the back door,
I peer into the kitchen:
brown cupboards and a tin drying rack
make it look like it was built before I was born,
and on the stove, a kettle.
A kettle boiling,
whistling for someone to
                    come quick, come quick,
                        and stop the steam from screaming.

Then I see her,
emerging from behind the fridge door,
                            face fragile and
                            filled with fear
                            when she spots me.

We stare.
            And do not move.

An Invitation

I bomb it
back down the garden
into the shed,
grab my bag
and
       go
go
     go.

I'm scrambling to get away
because I can't stay.

But.

Toffee?
A voice as quiet as pencil on paper.

The fencing won't let me through
no matter how hard I push,
                         pull,
                 and then
the voice again—
louder, possibly Irish.

Come back, for the love of Christ!
Toffee!

The woman holds up one hand
like a child in a classroom.
Toffee? she repeats for the third time,
an invitation, probably,
to come inside and eat something sweet.

Desperation spikes her tone.
And I know that feeling—
pleading with someone not to flee.

So.

Overflowing

The kitchen smells of toasted hot cross buns.
There's an empty plate of burned crumbs
on the counter.

I'd love one smothered in butter.

I can't turn off the water.
The woman
              points with her whole hand,
knotted fingers curled into her palm.
I can't turn the tap, she explains.
You'd think they'd make it easier.
We're not all beefcakes
but I wouldn't say no to one coming in
on a daily basis to turn those taps.
Jesus, let's be honest, he could turn more than my taps.
She winks, chuckles,
leads me through the kitchen
       to the hall,
              then a bathroom
              where a tub is
about to overflow onto the carpet tiles.
       I pull the plug, turn off the tap.

Water burbles and glugs.
A light bulb flickers.

I wanted to wash the nets.
But, you know, I'll throw them out.
I'd rather throw them than wash them.
Sure, who needs nets?

Not-quite-white net curtains rolled into a ball
    are piled high in the sink.

I gotta go.
I step back,
eyeball the front door.

The woman tilts her head to the side.
Can't you stay? she asks.
I'll get Mam to do another plate.
It's not like there'll be much to eat at your place.

Huh? No, I've got plans, I try,
but don't move,
    my body knowing more than my brain:
    I have no money and nowhere to go
    and leaving will mean traipsing in the rain.

The woman smiles,
showing off a set of tiny yellow snaggleteeth.
She is examining my face.

Does it hurt? she asks.

I touch the burn.
Yes, I admit. *A bit.*

She doesn't really look all that sorry but says,
I have ointment . . . Let me find it . . .
and shuffles back to the kitchen,
roots in a cupboard,
and hands me a bottle of SPF 30 sunscreen.
Is that what you were after? she asks.

I turn the bottle over, smile.
Um. Not exactly the weather for it, is it?

She looks irritated all of a sudden
like I am to blame.

My stomach pinches with hunger pangs.
Can I have a hot cross bun? I ask.

Oh yes,
    it's just like you to come over when you're hungry.
She pulls out a chair.
Now sit there.
Go on, sit there.

Hot Cross Buns

The crunch of the bread,
and melted butter

in my mouth at once.
anything

juice of the raisins
all mingling

I've never tasted
so good.

I Am Marla

What's your name? I ask.

She wags a finger accusingly,
then clouds over,
contemplating the question.
    I'm Marla.
    Yes.
    I am Marla.
    Now . . .

            did you hear back from Connor
    about the game on Saturday?
    Are we going or not?
    I can't stand the way he messes us 'round.
    Every bleedin' week it's the same old shite.
    He's a messer all right though. You know?
A pause. A glance at the window.
    The weather's turned, hasn't it?
    Felt like summer yesterday.
    I was meaning to plant some mint.
    Can you smell something burning
    or is it just me?

Hailstones, like little glass beads,
patter against the windowpanes.

Marla hands me a cherry ChapStick
and points to my cheek.
Try that.

Can I have another hot cross bun? I ask.

I Am Toffee

I tell Marla my real name,
twice:
      Allison. Allison.
And she uses it for a while,
      not looking at me,
then continues to call me Toffee.

She thinks that's who I am,
so I stop correcting her,
and anyway,
I like the idea of being
            sweet and hard,
            a girl with a name for people
            to chew on.

            A girl who could break teeth.

Bacon

I stare into Marla's bathroom mirror,
focus on my cooked and battered cheek.
I thought the redness would have faded by now,
the mark dissolved a bit,
but there it is,

                    blazing,

less like I've been burned
and more branded,
the color and shape of a slice of bacon
slapped against my face.

Behind me in the mirror Marla is
        watching,
her almost-not-there eyebrows furrow.
It looks awful. Let me help.

No, I snap,
not knowing what to do with her concern,
turning away so she sees less
of my wincing face in the mirror.

I don't need pity from this stranger.

The hurt is half my doing anyway.
 Stupid me.
 Stupid mouth.
 Stupid fault.

It'll fade.
Her voice is dashed with anger.
I don't remember it so brutal.

  She is wearing a ring with a bright blue
   sapphire.
  Her ears are studded with pearls.
  Both would sell for a decent amount.

My mouth gets stuck.
I blink.
I better go, I tell her.

  I step into the hallway.

  A leather handbag is hanging
   unbuckled
   from the
   newel post.

Marla shakes her head. Looks sad.
It'd be deadly if you stayed.
We could play poker. Ah, don't go, Toff.

I'll stay until the worst of the weather passes.

A mound of loose change is
lying in an ashtray.

The forecast
predicts rain
for days.

Hobnobs

We watch a talk show, the news,
eat Hobnobs and drink tea.
At ten o'clock Marla's phone beeps.
                    That's me, then.
She switches off the TV.

When I was doing my exams
I used a reminder to tell me
to go to sleep too, I say,
speaking more than I have all evening.

                    Oh, I have reminders for everything.
                    I mightn't remember otherwise, she says.
                    She peers at the phone.
                    Peggy put them in.
                    Good night then.
                    Are you going now?
                    I'm shattered.

Yes, it's late.

                    She nods and leaves,
        switching off the lights on her way to bed.

Without knowing why,
I tiptoe up the stairs
after Marla,
my ear against her door,
listening,
pushing on another door, where
a bedroom is revealed—
    the bed stripped bare,
    walls painted avocado.

    No one else lives here.
    That's obvious.
    So I could have one night.
        What harm would one night do?

I dash downstairs
and in the kitchen stare out at the shed.
But instead of leaving,
        I lock the doors
and return
to the avocado
bedroom.

Victory

Every hour I do not call my father
is a victory,
a declaration:
> I do not need you.
> I do not want to be with you.

Although,
   the longer it goes on,
   the more I get to wondering
whether his silence
means
exactly the same thing.

Alarm Bell

I am blasted out of sleep by an alarm
and scramble downstairs
in only a T-shirt and underwear.
    Nee-awwwwwwwww,
    nee-awwwwwwwww.

The kitchen is a fog of toasty smoke.
Marla is in her nightie, teetering on a stool,
frantically flapping a tea towel at a fire alarm
on the ceiling.

I grab a newspaper,
wave it around
until the noise stops,
then grab Marla by the wrist, help her
hobble down from the stool.

Who in blazes are you? she asks.
Why aren't you wearing a skirt?

I hesitate.
I got here yesterday.
I'm leaving in a minute.
Sorry.

She stares at my feet,
the purple nail polish worn away
at the tips of my toenails
from too-tight shoes.
Did you burn the toast? It wasn't me.
She sounds suspicious.
I don't even like toast. I like rolls with butter.

The fridge door is open.
                On one shelf
                a small stack
                of paperback books:
                        Jane Austen,
                        Emily Brontë,
                        Danielle Steel.

I could eat the twelve apostles though, she says.
Did you pick up sausages?
I'd kill for some mash.

It is six fifteen in the morning.
My eyes are sandy;
my stomach is sore.
Before I get out of here I could do with some food,
because I can't stay—
                she's clearly out of her mind.

I'll make sausage sandwiches, I say.
You see what's on the TV.

She heads for the metal bread box.
I can butter something. I'm not useless.
She bites her thumbnail
      and scans the kitchen.
Who are you anyway?
Do Mary and Donal know you're here?
Is Peggy on her way or not?

I'm here from city council, I tell her,
clutching her elbow and
leading her to the sitting room.

City council? Don't give me that.
City council didn't send you here wearing no clothes.
Do you think I'm batty?
Is Peggy okay?
She squares up to me.
Her breath is full of sleep.

I go back into the kitchen to prepare the sausages.
She follows and stands watching,
      watching me make breakfast
in my underwear.

Who Did That to Your Face?

She asks.

No One Did Anything to Me

I tell her.

Home Help

I am zipping up my jeans
when a voice rings out.
Marla! It's Peggy!
The front door slams shut.

I can't get my feckin' tights on, Marla shouts
from the bedroom next to mine.
My arse has expanded.

Feet pad the stairs.
I nudge my room door closed
and press an ear against it.

Your mouth never stops expanding either.
You not dressed yet? I messaged to remind you.
The woman, Peggy, laughs and starts to whistle,
     noise nothing like a melody.

They sent someone else, Marla says.
A young thing.
Lovely, she is.
Almost burned the house down around me.

A pause.

Is someone after my job? Peggy asks.
Was she funnier than I am?
Did she climb in a window?

Marla doesn't reply because
these are not real questions.
They are condescensions.

Peggy doesn't believe a word Marla's saying,
hearing only confusion
                      not facts.

She must have a key, Marla says.
Or maybe she was here all night.
She was in her knickers.

Noises come from the other room
that sound like fussing, sorting, tidying.
Well, I'll definitely look
to make sure she left.
Peggy is completely unconvinced.
Sorry I was late.
There was a tractor in front of me the whole way
from Stratton and he wouldn't pull over.
What a headache!

I scramble around the room,

squeezing things into my bag,
  then quietly
  slide beneath the bed,
press my side against a collection
of dusty hatboxes.

Eventually the room door does open;
heavy white sneakers appear,
  tidily laced to the top.
No one in the spare room, Marla! Peggy calls out.
  Her feet are still.
Then she bends,
  hair covering her face,
and collects a sock I missed
from the carpet.
We should probably give it a clean in here.
  And she is gone,
out the door again, calling,
Have you had your Jolly Ranchers yet?

Jolly Ranchers?

Your meds, woman. Your meds.
I'll find them. You come on down
when you've put your face on.

In my pocket, my phone vibrates.

I Check My Phone

Finally a message from Kelly-Anne.
    Oh My God. Where r u????
I type only one word.
    Bude

Later

See you tomorrow! Peggy shouts.

I peep out the window.
Peggy is a wide woman.
She slams Marla's front gate shut
and climbs into a car too tiny for her,
      the side-view mirror attached with tape.

I tiptoe down the stairs
with all my stuff.
In the hall Marla's handbag
is still dangling from the newel post.
I take from it her wallet
and then a ten,
      plastic-smooth,
put the wallet back again.

And then I am running
out the back door
heading for the seashore.

Birdbrain

A man on the beach is taunting a seagull,
mocking the bird's swagger, mimicking its squawk,
while he uses a metal detector
to search for pieces of copper
worth less than a bag of chips.

A woman reads with earbuds in
while a pair of toddling twins
hit each other with sandy spades.

A couple lie on a towel too close to the sea,
sharing kisses and germs.

I leave my belongings in a pile,
stuff my socks into my shoes,
and go to the shore.

      The smarting sea
strokes my feet
      and I would like to feel
that freeze throughout my body,
      but I am dressed in jeans and a sweater
and cannot dive in like the dog nearby,
      who yaps and bites at the waves.

And then the rain comes,
heavy with wind.
Sand scratches my skin.

I return to my things.

But.

My backpack has gone
and with it all
    my spare clothes,
        my phone,
            a KitKat I stole from Marla.
Shit.
Bastards.
Bollocks.
Shit shit shit.

I run along the beach,
    empty
now apart from the metal detector man.
He stops,
holds opens his hand to flaunt a find:
one golden hooped earring.
Luck is everything.
You just have to know when it's your day, he says.

Lipstick

Dad found lipstick in my school bag
and confronted me with it.
What's this?
I didn't have an answer.
The previous week he'd caught me reading
Kelly-Anne's *Cosmopolitan* and tore it in two.
Do you have a boyfriend? he asked,
not completely unkindly.

No, Daddy.

So what's the face paint about?

I don't know.
And the truth was, I didn't.
I'd used it once or twice
but didn't see much point
when it just wiped off a few minutes later.

He took a deep breath.
I'm being very patient here, Allison.
But don't push me. Okay?

I wiped my mouth with my sleeve
even though I was sure
I didn't have anything on my lips.
Okay, Daddy.

Sweetness

The shops are shutting,
metal grates pulled down and padlocked
to stop windows from being smashed,
stuff from getting stolen.
A woman is locking up a candy shop—
      fudge displayed in colorful rows,
        left exposed to tempt passersby.
Her hair is piled up high like icing on a cupcake.
She smiles when she sees me
then steps close.
I can smell her sugary scent.
You all right there, darling?
She looks up at the unfriendly sky,
back into my face,
quickly away again.

      I had forgotten about my face.

Is there a hostel in town?

You mean for backpackers or for . . . ?

She is unable to gauge my age—
      undecided about whether or not to worry.

I'm traveling, I tell her.
Her smile widens in relief.

It's what I'm used to—
　　telling lies and observing how
　　people untighten
　　when they aren't required to care.

Teachers were this way.
Is everything okay at home, Allison?
　　they'd ask, only half looking up
　　from their marking.
When I nodded eagerly, it was enough to
absolve them.

The candy woman is pointing.
Your best bet is a B and B along Summerleaze Crescent.
This time of year you'll get something good.
Quite cheap.

Oh, yes, I'll find somewhere to stay.

Dawdle

I shouldn't dawdle.

I need to look like I have a goal,
seem to be going somewhere.
       As soon as I don't,
       I'm spotted.
Hey, sweetheart, give us a smile.
The man slows his car so he can
       follow me.
Wanna lift? Jump in.
       I move quicker up the hill.
Where are you going anyway?
Is someone expecting you?
Get in. I don't bite, sweetheart.
He is stopped by a red light
and I rush
out of sight
down an alleyway,
       running, running, running,
until I find the end
and a road I recognize as Marla's.

A man walking a dog sidesteps me.
A car horn somewhere sounds loudly.

Rattle

The window in the shed rattles.
Rain pounds the roof.

I sit in the dark,
crunched into a small ball
to protect me from the cold.

I have to admit,
when I left
I imagined something
better than this.

And now,
I have no phone,
so Kelly-Anne will never find me.

Birthday

Kelly-Anne woke me early.
Get up, lazybones. It's your birthday!

She'd made French toast
topped with whipped cream and berries.

Next to my breakfast, a package.
An archery set I'd talked about for ages.

It wasn't a real one—suckers instead of points
at the ends of the arrows.

But she'd bought window chalk too,
drawn a target in various colors across the glass.

We spent all day shooting at that window,
perfecting our aim.

I guess we were learning to arm ourselves.
We were learning how to fight.

And we were always on the same side.

Disregard

Marla inspects a lavender bush
potted on the patio.
I watch from the window in the shed.
Peggy is behind her in the kitchen, busy.

Marla mutters something.

Peggy shouts. *What? What did you say?*

When's Mary coming? Marla shouts,
                            much louder than necessary.
I need to get some bits in—
at least make up a few sandwiches.
She was like one of those skateboarders
last time she was here.
You'd give her a penny.

I smile, not completely understanding
Marla's expressions,
knowing Peggy probably won't either.

Marla rubs the lavender
between thumb and forefinger,
brings the scent to her nose.

She looks toward the shed.
I freeze.

Peggy steps outside.
Eggs, she announces,
guiding Marla away from the plant
without a hint of interest
in anything Marla has just said.

A wasp follows them into the house.

A Companion

Marla might talk to Peggy about me
but Peggy will not hear her
and
will not
        be able to protect her from any
intruder
invader
burglar
thief.

I could be a ghost.

I could be a Toffee
or a Tara
or a Clara
or a Claire
or anything else the old woman wants.
        It isn't as though Allison was ever allowed
        anyway.
        She could be very quiet,
                        almost invisible.

I have known worse compromises
than forfeiting a name.

I could stay.

No one would believe Marla
if she cried foul play.

They'd smirk and vow
to inspect the place.

They would say she was mad.

If I stayed I could take what I needed
and no one
would stop me.

Forgotten

Do not come down those stairs until I say so,
do you hear me?
His face was blood-filled, hard, veins popping
in his neck.

Yes, Daddy.
I scuttled away
so he couldn't get to me.

I missed lunch.
I missed dinner.
As he left for work the next morning
I opened the door   an inch
            then closed it again.

        By the evening
                my stomach was stinging.

Allie? Dad called up the stairs.
You home from school?

I rushed onto the landing.
I've been in my bedroom, I told him.
You said I wasn't supposed to leave.

He sucked his teeth.
You're a real idiot
sometimes, you know that?

Back

I ease open
        the back door.
Marla is jabbing a radio
with a screwdriver,
scowling.
I can't get the bloody thing to work.
Why are there so many buttons?
Does it need batteries?
I can't find any.
She glances up.
You aren't Peggy.

I consider telling the truth,
        though
                only for a nanosecond.

I'm Toffee.
I form the fakest smile I can muster.
        It's not like I haven't had a lot of practice
        being a pretender:
        I know how happiness should look
        from the outside.

Marla tilts her head.

Don't just stand there then.

Fix the bleedin' thing.

Fruit

In the fruit bowl are two lemons
and a soft apple
along with
shiny coins
and a crisp bill.

I pocket the money
and put on the kettle.

The System

Dad liked to beat the system
     and other people too sometimes.
When I needed new jeans
we walked into H&M
and he went straight to the men's section,
taking a checkered shirt from a peg,
pulling off the top button,
and marching to the cashier.

I stood next to him, not listening,
     wondering if I could take a mint
     from the bowl on the counter.
     No, I haven't got the receipt
        but it's damaged,
        isn't it?
        You can see for yourself.
        Look.
        See?
        Look there.
She quietly made him an offer.
     No, I want my money back.
And another offer.
     No, I don't wanna exchange it.

The girl at the register was hardly older than I was—
　　hair in long braids,
　　　　green eyeliner—
　　　　and I knew how it felt,
　　　　　　to be bombarded by him.

The best I can do is a credit note, she mumbled.
My manager isn't back from lunch for an hour.

Dad drummed his fingers against the counter
and agreed,
slipping the card with the money on it
into my hand
as we walked away.

Get yourself the jeans, he said.
I'll be in the car. Hurry up.

It was the kindest thing he'd done in ages,
and it made me remember to love him.

Moon Tiger

Marla's bookshelves are lined
with paperbacks—
     classics, poetry, romance, crime,
the spines bent and broken,
pages yellow and weak.

I curl up under a lamp,
reading a book called *Moon Tiger*,
mouthing the words
like a prayer
while Marla sits looking into her lap,
suddenly spent,
quiet,
withdrawn.

     I have no idea what she is feeling
     and this not knowing makes me shift in my
     chair constantly.

Eventually her phone pings
and it rouses her—
her mind wriggling back into the room.
Bedtime.

At the door she turns.
Are you going home?

Yes. Soon.
I hold the book aloft.

She nods in a sort of expressionless way
and heads upstairs,
        flushes the toilet,
        shuts her bedroom door.

In the half-lit room
I sit with *Moon Tiger*
until sleepiness creeps through me
and I can't keep my eyes open
for the last chapters.

        Electricity buzzes in the room.
        Something crackles.
        But Marla does not return.
        She stays asleep.

And here I am alone in her home,
reading her books,
pretending to be someone I am not.

She will see through me tomorrow.
But I suppose that doesn't matter tonight.

I have a bed
and the doors in this house
are locked tight.

I can't go home.
So I am staying.

Too Long

I hadn't known he was in a hurry
until he was
             behind me in my room,
glaring back at me in the full-length mirror.
I've been waiting, he said.

Kelly-Anne loitered on the landing.
             Is it cold out?
             Are either of you taking coats?
             She was wearing a new dress.

Dad ignored her.

Nearly ready, I said,
running a brush through my hair
to the ends,
tying it up high onto my head.

             Are you taking a coat? Kelly-Anne asked again.
             She was in the room now, next to Dad.

He stormed out.
             She made a face.

Dad returned
        with a pair of scissors,
and before I could jerk my head from him
he had hold
of my ponytail
and was cutting it,
        cutting it,
        cutting it,
until he was holding the whole length of my hair
in his hands.
        Kelly-Anne gasped. *Marcus!*

Too long, he muttered.

I nodded.
But I didn't know what was too long:
the amount of time I'd made him wait
or the length of hair
        he'd just stolen from me.

Cleaner

As I come out of the toilet,
Marla sees me and screams.
　　　Who are you?
She covers her face with her fingers
for protection.

I step into the hall light,
holding up my hands,
about to tell her
　　　I am Toffee.

Marla steps back.
Who are you?

　　　I stare at her.
　　　Who am I?
　　　Who? Who?
　　　Think, Allison, think.

I was just here to clean, I mutter.
I sit at the bottom of the stairs and
slip on my sneakers.
Cobwebs hang beneath the hall table.

Marla reaches for an umbrella,
waves it at me.
I don't need a cleaner.
Don't come back here.
I'm well able to do my own polishing.

I understand.

She holds the umbrella aloft,
and clumsily,
unluckily,
it opens.

I step closer.
I haven't been paid.
I hold out my palm.

She seems to smirk at my audacity.
Do I look like a bleedin' cripple?
I'm not.
I can push a broom around the place
and I'd break someone's back with it
if they messed me about,
     don't think I wouldn't.
You haven't been cleaning.

I'm owed twelve quid, I tell her.
I've got no idea why I'm insisting,
why I don't just go away
and come back later.

She chews her tongue.

Your handbag's in the sitting room.
My voice is lined with ridicule,
my expression hard.
   Leave, I tell myself.
   What the hell are you doing?

You aren't getting any money from me.
She isn't messing around.

I march past her
into the sitting room,
where I collect her bag
then come back out and hand it to her.
Twelve. Pounds.

My knees are shaking although
she is watching me less confidently,
perhaps with a thread of fear.
How many hours were you here?

Two. It's six pounds per hour.

She looks up at the ceiling,
puts the open umbrella aside.
I don't want you back here, madam.
Don't let me see you in this house again.
You hear me?
If I see you back I'll get the guards.
Don't think I won't.
She glances at the rotary telephone.
It is black, dusty.

I shrug.
She hands me a ten and two coins.

See you later, I say.

Caught

I don't have a waterproof coat,
and quickly it goes from cloudy to torrential,
    rain sweeping across the sky in
    thick panels.

Cold comes in from the ocean.
My cheek stings.

I wedge myself between
    two lopsided beach huts
to keep dry
and look up
only when a pair of Hunter rain boots
    comes to a halt in front of me.

A girl with a silky Labrador frowns down.
The dog's tail wags,
        flicks rain.
Water drips from the hem of the girl's hood.
    Are you hurt? she asks.
    What happened to your face?

Just got caught in the rain, I say.

Beach Hut Number 13

The beach hut has its back to the town,
                face to the sea,
a full view of the Atlantic—
a straight line all the way to America
if you had the guts to get going.

The wood smells of mint and mold.

I could live here, I murmur to the girl,
who is drying off the dog with a dishcloth.

She laughs,
tells me about the time her brother
moved in
for a week,
when he was studying for his exams
and couldn't stand the sound of drumming.
Who plays the drums? I ask.

I do, she says casually,
like that sort of thing could be ordinary.

Her name is Lucy,
and she speaks

as though the world has always listened to her.
I can't look her in the eye.

I examine the floorboards,
scrutinize the dog's paws and
the jellyfish-patterned rug.

She glances up at the mute roof.
It's stopped raining, she says,
which I take to mean,
You can leave now.

So I do.

Friends

Dad didn't like me having friends.
He said,

> *If I pay for your swimming,*
> *you'll think things come easy.*
> *They don't.*
> *Make yourself useful.*
> *Start with that dishwasher.*

He said,

> *You can get a Saturday job*
> *when you've finished your exams.*
> *I'm a decent father. Don't you eat?*

He said,

> *It's too late to go out.*
> *You think I don't know what goes on?*

I could have invited friends over to the house
but also
     I couldn't.

Sophie and Jacq weren't the sort of girls to
     keep mum if things were weird—
     Jacq was a worrier, Sophie was a chatterbox.

I didn't want them seeing how he was,
huffing and angry,
cruel to Kelly-Anne.

Why didn't you come to Martin's? Jacq asked.
He likes you 'cause he went on and on.
His brother's got a new motorbike.
Said he'll let us have a go next time.
Gotta be careful what you wear though
in case you set fire to your leg on the exhaust.

Allie thinks she's too good for us, Sophie said.
You already got a boyfriend or something?
What's his name? Is it Jacq's dad?

Shut up, said Jacq.
　　　She pushed Sophie.
　　　They laughed.
Jacq's dad was living with a twenty-year-old
　　　in some hovel.
We pretended his girlfriend was still in elementary
　　　school,
that her dad was a weirdo.
Jacq pretended to find it funny.

I wanted to come out, I told them.
Dad's being a pain.

So *come Saturday*, Jacq said.
We'll go down to the movies.
                    Sneak in.
Nothing worth paying for anyway.
Jacq held on longer than Sophie,
tried really hard to keep me from

                                        slipping
                                        away.

I can't.
I didn't have an explanation.
The only reason for not hanging out
was that I was scared.
But even then,
I couldn't exactly explain
what I was afraid he might do.

Waiting

Marla is sitting at the kitchen table
giving a crossword puzzle the evil eye,
a lidded pen between her fingers.
I rap on the woodwork so she won't be startled.
I'm back, I say,
    as casually as I can,
    hoping she'll remember me as Toffee
    not the counterfeit cleaner
    so I can stay.
Oh, she murmurs, without excitement.
        I need help with six across.
        Abode: four letters.

I fiddle with my sleeve,
pull it over my fingers.
Home, I whisper.

    She counts the tiny boxes.
    You're home.
    Yes. Home. Okay.

Crosswords

Everything Dad ever said was a puzzle,
    blanks and clues,
    words crossing
      v
      e
    horizontally,
      t
      i
      c
      a
      l
      l
      y,
the answers never evident.

Crosswords I can do.
But I could never work out my father.

Tired

It was just noise.
Loud noise that did nothing.
Loud noise that sounded around me
then   vanished.
So why did I shake when he shouted?
Allison! Allison?
How many times have I told you
not to leave your shoes lying around?
I knew my school shoes were next to the couch
'cause I kicked them off to read,
        and my sneakers were still in the bathroom,
        where I'd left them after my shower.
        It was before Kelly-Anne came to live with us
        and taught me how to keep out of his way.
                I was seven maybe.
                I wet the bed sometimes.
Allison? Do your shoes need their own place?
Allison? Where are you?
Not clearing up, that's for sure.
He was clomping up the stairs,
        heavy-footed.
I don't ask much, do I?
I mean, do I ask for much?

A tidy house isn't a lot to ask for.
Is it?
Is it?
The walls rattled.
The ceilings came closer.
I stepped onto the landing.
I'm sorry, Daddy.
I'll do it now.
I was crying.
There was snot.
Choking sounds came from my throat.
And he relented,
just like that,
head tilted like he was working me out.
Jesus, Al, I'm so tired.
That's all it is.
Don't snivel. Come on, gimme a break.
We're buddies, aren't we?

He could have hugged me then
to show he hadn't meant to shout,
to show what love felt like,
                    but he didn't.
He opened his own bedroom door,

kicked his shoes and clothes across the floor,
and fell down onto his bed to sleep.

And that's the thing.
        He hadn't lied.
He really had been very tired.

During the Commercial Break

Marla dozes for a few minutes.

When she opens her eyes she is afraid.
Where's Mary? she asks.
She presses herself into her chair.

I don't know where she is.
I hold up my hands in surrender.

I'm starved.
She points as though I'm the one
who's starved her.

Well, I can make you something.
What do you want?

I want Mary. *Who are you at all?*
I want my Mary.

I'm Toffee.

Marla squints and smiles,
forgetting her growling stomach.

For a moment she looks young;
her face is bright, body bouncy.

Toffee! Oh, we should practice!

Practice what? I ask.

You're making fun of me.
Either that, or you've had a bump on the head.

Marla Has Moves

Marla
 grooves and swivels,
 jiggles and jives,
not afraid of the high tempo
or the possibility she could trip and
knock herself against the stone mantelpiece.
Come on, Toff, keep up!
Roger said we need to be ready.
I hear Moira's ready. And Frances.
Those bitches.
Move, Toffee!
She drags me by the arm to join her,
hip dipping one way, then the other,
music roaring around the room
from the record player.
And once the song ends,
needle in a little crane
lifting itself off the spinning record,
she starts the whole thing over.

Routine

Right foot forward,
        right foot back,
quick, quick, quick,
        slow—slow,
point to the sky, and spin,
right foot
right foot
right foot
right,
wink at the crowd, and grin.

And again but faster:
left foot now,
quick, quick, quick,
        slow—slow,
left foot back, and dip,
left foot
left foot
left foot
left,
wiggle three times, and skip.

Strictly

Dad worked weekends,
    taxiing drunks from pub to club,
    charging extra if they puked in his car.

It meant the sitting room was free,
    and the TV,
so Kelly-Anne and I ordered pizza
and watched *Dancing with the Stars*,
phoned up to vote for our favorites,
watched the best bits
again on repeat.

Once we pretended to tango,
    bodies pressed close,
    arms outstretched,
        strutting from one end of the room
        to the other
        and back again.

Dad finished early that evening,
was watching us for ages before
we noticed him
    there
    by the sideboard,

recording us with his phone.
Oh, don't stop on my account, he said.

But we did.
　　We stepped away from each other,
　　ashamed of our friendship,
　　ashamed of the fun.

We were just messing about, Kelly-Anne said.

Dad pinched the end of his nose.
Must be nice to have time for that.

I turned off the TV and went to the kitchen
to make Dad's dinner.
He followed me in.
Someone's been sick in the car.
You'll have to clean it.

I nodded and found the rubber gloves.

Kelly-Anne and I didn't dance again.

The Hunt

When I know Marla is asleep,
I hunt for traces of Toffee,
rummage through drawers, cupboards,
tip shoeboxes onto my lap, and
scan black-and-white photographs,
newspaper cuttings for clues.

In the darkness,
I search through pieces of the past
to find a way to jigsaw Toffee together again,
make myself a girl who was.

Instead I find Marla—
    in hats and ruffles,
    hair puffed up like a well-baked sponge cake.
    Marla with long, slim legs,
    eyes bright,
    mouth curled at the corners
    as though suppressing laughter when the
        camera
            clicked.

But then one picture makes me
    pause,

stare into history:
    Marla is arm-linked to another girl,
    both in minidresses,
    hair to their hips,
    and this girl,
    Toffee it must be,
        this girl,
        she is me.

Toffee

A scar on her face like a stubborn stain,
eyes peering into the lens,
pleading
pleading
pleading
with someone,
      with anyone,
            with a girl from the future,
      to see her.

Scars

Was Toffee's stain
    something assigned to her from Day One,
    a birthmark she had owned for life
    and learned not to see
    when she looked at herself?

Or, like me,
    did someone give her that scar,
    change her face from ordinary to ugly
    with one strong swing?

When Toffee looked at herself
    did she see the scar,
    a girl,
    or the person hurting her?

Out

OUT! she screams.

I am doing dishes.
I wipe my wet hands on my jeans.
What's happened, Marla?

The house had been quiet,
only the exhaust fan
above the stove
whirring.

She points and spits
        like a rabid dog.
Out! Out! Out! Out!

For the first time
I am afraid of her,
of what she could do.
I'm leaving.

OUT!

I'm leaving.

OUT! OUT!

I push past her,
kick a chair,
which topples.
Have fun alone, I murmur.

What did you say? she hisses.

It isn't like you're inundated with visitors,
      is it?
My voice is louder than I want it to be,
      louder than I would have raised it with Dad,
and it's pointless because she
can't help it.

Who are you? She is genuinely puzzled,
an old woman with an intruder in her home
simply trying to protect herself.

I have no idea, I tell her.

OUT! she shouts. *OUT!*

Fictional

I stop at Hal's Fish and Chip Shop,
order a battered cod.

A group of girls comes in,
     pushing each other,
     screeching.
I can't believe he replied, says one.
I know. What a tool, says another.
     Pushing. Screeching.
You getting fries? says one.
Can't I share yours? says another.

I pay for my fish and am eating at a window seat
when Lucy comes in with the dog.
The girls call her over.
     Nick is so rude!
     But she liked it anyway.
     Lucy, you going to Kate's place Sunday?
     Kate's a bitch, Lucy says.
     She is, they all reply.

Lucy spots me. Says nothing. Goes to the counter.
     Keep your number private if you don't
     wanna get messaged, she says to the girls,

and orders a bag of fries.
Nick's a total stalker.
Kate's so getting dumped.
They make sounds of approval.

I leave half the food on the plate
and pull on my coat.
I am almost at the corner when she catches up.
You didn't have to go, she says.

I was finished, I tell her.

No, I mean from the hut the other day.
We could have . . .
I don't know . . .
You could have told me your name
before you ran off.
Bit abnormal, wasn't it?
But maybe you are abnormal.
Most people are bonkers.
I am. But in a good way.
Healthy levels of weird right here.
What's your name then?

I blink and think.
My name?

Am I Allison or Toffee?
And what about this girl with Lucy?
Who is she?

I could take a name from history—
            a woman who stepped into herself
            without asking permission.
I could be Coco Chanel or Rosa Parks.
I could be my mother,
                        Davina Daniels.

But all these people are dead
and I usually want to be alive.

I try to imagine a living woman—
            someone strong—
            but my mind is a blank,
            filled only with pictures of
            people running away
            or struggling to stay put.
Juliet, I tell her,
            deciding on someone fictional,
            dead because her dad was an asshole.

The Labrador is pulling at the lead,
tugging on Lucy's arm.

She doesn't resist.

Soon she is far ahead.
Juliet! she shouts.
Like from Macbeth?

I laugh,
though I can't be sure she is joking.

Research

I find the thinnest of books,
    sit with it in a corner,
    hunched over the pages,
ignoring the rhyme-time-baby-cry-zone
happening at the library's opposite end.

Before I'm even halfway through the book
I'm pretty sure it's dementia Marla's got.

So I need to be calm.
I need to smile, explain things,
say her name when we speak,
and
    stop,
    focus on her with my full attention.

If I want to find a way to stay put
for a while,
    I'll need to understand the illness—
        understand her.

And although some part of my brain
tells me I could be there to help Marla,
I know I am only helping myself,

there for Allison's sake
alone.

A Range Rover in the parking lot
makes sloppy attempts
to fit into a too-small space.
      I leave the book on the windowsill
      and leave the library.

Good Girl

I didn't know when I was little
that what went on at home was a
                    secret.

I didn't know I shouldn't
tell tales to teachers.
Instead I babbled
and a social worker came
to our house
dressed in baggy clothes
and covered in cat hair.

She looked at my bedroom.
        Dad had changed the sheets
        and vacuumed the rug.
She saw the house was tidy,
the fridge full,
and I had no bruises.

She talked to Dad
        in a soft voice
and was satisfied:
the shouting
I'd tattled about was normal,

the smacking was hasty and would
stop
now that Dad knew the rules.

Keep these buttoned, Dad said
when she left,
pinching my lips between his fingers.

Yes, Daddy.

Good girl, he said, and smiled.
I liked it when he did that,
                    when he smiled
                    because of me.

How Long?

How long will the school hold off
before pestering Dad about my absence?
Will they call the police if he shuffles, stammers,
　　　says he isn't sure where I am?

And how will Dad prove to anyone
I left willingly
and am not
buried in the garden?

Perhaps he is searching the streets
trying to find me,
reach me,
bring me back.

I don't want him to discover me here,
but I want him to try—
　　　to be sad
　　　he has lost me.

Yet.

Sometimes I think,
      if only
      he *had* just buried me in the garden.

Everything would be easier.

And How Long?

How many times has Kelly-Anne tried to call?
And how many more times will she do the same?

I've made her worry,
when she has worries enough.
So how long before she gives up?

How long before Kelly-Anne washes her hands
of everything she made herself be to me?

How long before she forgets me entirely?

And how long before I stop wanting her?

Transparent

Every drawer Marla opens makes her grunt.
Every cupboard makes her scream.
Every chair, shove;
      every door, elbow.
Can I help? I ask.

Where are the tea bags? she shouts.

I go to the counter,
      open a ceramic pot,
      blackberries painted on the side,
      and hold up what she's looking for.

Makes no sense.
That's fruit.
That should have fruit in it.

And she's right.
The coffee container has gooseberries on the side;
the sugar container, pears.

Makes no sense, she repeats.

I find tall glass tumblers above the sink,

fill three with
tea, coffee, sugar,
and pop them on the countertop.
You'll know where they are now.

Marla grins
with as little of her mouth as possible.
Smart arse. Boil the kettle then.

Okay So

I have nothing to wear so I search Marla's
wardrobe for something that doesn't
seem utterly ridiculous.

Downstairs in her cream blouse
and mustard-colored cardigan
I wait for her to say something—
accuse me or at the very least
laugh.

She looks me up and down.
Smirks.
Well, okay so, is all she says.
　　　Okay so.

Miscalculations

Lucy is crouching beside her
Grape-colored beach hut,
scribbling something onto the concrete
with a piece of chalk.

Her dog bounds from the hut,
licks my knee.

Lucy stands.
The skin on her lips is dry;
a vertical crack on the bottom lip bleeds a little.
You're back.
She points to the ground—
a scrawl of numbers and letters
                    under her feet.
*It's algebra. Also known as
complete and utter crap.
Got about four hundred
equations to get done.*

You can't hand that in.

She finds her phone and snaps some photos.

Actually, I believe in impermanence.
I'm pretty into philosophy.

Right.
I stare down at a miscalculated equation,
wondering whether to swipe the chalk, correct her.

I'm bullshitting.
I just like pissing off my math teacher.
He's a dick. And he's doing the vice principal.

I scuff at her scrawl with the toe of my sneaker.
Her dog sniffs my feet.

I've got a load of history to do too
but I'll wait and write that up on my laptop
like a normal person.
She pauses.
Your face looks pretty sore.

> *I'm fine.*
> I paste my hair
> across my cheek
> to cover it.

Do you wanna go somewhere?

I clutch the coins in my pocket,
my last four quid.
If we can walk then yeah.

Cool. I know a great place for kissing.

      I stare.

It's a joke. Relax.
It's a joke.

A Great Place for Kissing

The lighthouse really would be the perfect place
        if you had someone to kiss:
candy-cane column
wedged into craggy rocks,
        tall waves growling
then backing off
when the reply
is solid and silent.

Lolly loves it here.
Lucy ruffles the dog's fur.
Her arms are goose-bumpy.

The sky is overcast,
rumbling in argument with itself.
Feels like you could get eaten alive,
swallowed up, I say.
A seagull squawks
        and inches toward the ocean.
I will the water to cover me,
take me to the sea,
and hold me down until
everything is silent.

Until time has mended the world.

My boyfriend broke up with me, Lucy says suddenly.
Went off with my best friend, Kate.
I already guessed.
Found her bus pass in his coat. Slut.

Oh. I'm sorry. Do you miss him?

She laughs.
Nah.
He looks like a ferret.
It's my friend I lost.
She stares at her hands,
        pauses, and shouts, *Lolly!*
In seconds the dog is beside us—
        wet and gasping.
You stink. She reattaches his lead.

Did you talk to your boyfriend like that? I ask.
'Cause if you did, maybe he was right to
run off with someone else.

She side-eyes me
and I realize she isn't Sophie or Jacq,

who could take any joke
you hurled at them.

I better go. She stands.
I'm at the beach hut a lot
        after school
if you wanna come over.
You don't have anywhere to be? she asks.

The tide is rising.
I'm a siren, I say. *I've got sailors to drown.*

I sit by the lighthouse for a long time,
        allow the water to drench me.

        I am cold.
        I am alone.

        I am unkissed.

Unkissed

I have never been kissed.

Not on the mouth
or cheek or
top of the head

I don't think.

Dad patted me, never pecked,
when I'd been good as a kid.

And by the time
Kelly-Anne appeared
I was too old for her
lips
and made do with high fives
and the occasional cuddle.

I have never been kissed.

Bloody

Red splotches on the linoleum.
Smudged fingerprints smeared on the doors.
Marla?

She is slumped in the hallway,
hand over her nose,
face sticky with blood.
The press in the kitchen came at me, she says.
A poltergeist for all I know.
I need an ambulance.

My heart pumps hard.
How will I explain to a paramedic who I am
and why I found her?
Will they assume I did something awful?
Marla won't remember what happened.
Let me look.
I press her head to feel for bumps.
Her hair is matted with dried blood.
Can you stand up?

I don't feel magical.
I might need a doctor.

I get her to a chair.
I'll run you a bath, I say.

A bath will be a distraction.

Eggshells

Marla is watchful,
glancing at me now and again
as though waiting for me to speak.
I stay quiet,
not wanting to make her mad
or confused
or throw me out again.

I have left stepping on eggshells
for stepping on eggshells.

With one difference.

Marla hasn't hurt me.

When the Sun Comes Out

I arrange a tray
and take it into the garden,
where Marla and I sit in our coats
nibbling on buns and sipping lemonade.
It's a weedy mess out here, she says.
Mam's usually so good at keeping up with the garden.

Let's tidy it, I suggest.

Marla lifts a glass to her lips.
We can plant anything we want.
Let's get some sunflower seeds!
Or we could grow vegetables.
How about cabbage?

Dad would disapprove.
He'd think it was
bullshit
to grow your own food.
Yes. Let's try cabbage, I say.

Clearing Up

Marla wears a sun hat and too-big gardening gloves.
She starts by weeding the patio
but can't bend for long,
goes inside for water.
I cover myself over in her old nightie and get busy
picking pieces of broken glass from the grass,
stones from dead flower beds.
I can't see much progress
even after a couple of hours
but Marla is smiling.
       It's lovely this garden, isn't it? It's lovely.
I'm not sure she can remember what it was before
but she seems to know what it is now
and is happy.

Which is the main thing.

What Is Left Over

Peggy leaves food covered in foil
for each evening meal.

Usually
Marla wanders into the kitchen and
eats straight from the carton.

But tonight she forgets
so I serve her food
                    on a tray
                    with a glass of orange juice
                    diluted down with a little water.
Marla doesn't ask where the
food has come from
and, when finished,
passes the tray to me like I'm a waiter,
like I have always been there.
Thank you.

She doesn't eat much,
        leaves potatoes on her plate
        that look too good to waste.

I eat what is left over.

Mercy

I baked potatoes with tuna and corn.
Dad curled his nose
like I'd piled the plate
with dirty underwear.
You can't even get the easy stuff right, he said.

I try, I told him.

He raised his hand at this retort
then changed his mind.
> *You make it very hard to love you,*
> *you know,*
> *Allie.*

At times he could be merciful.

Love

If you could learn to be lovable
like you can learn to play the piano
or conjugate verbs,
my report would read:

Must try harder.

Washing Dishes

When I went to the bathroom,
Dad started on the dishes.
He'd scraped the cold potato into the trash
and was scrubbing the pan clean.
I can do that, I said.

He smiled.
Nah. It's my turn.
And, hey, the dinner was fine.
I'm just a grump.

I didn't reply.
I set to drying the plates,
asking myself if his changed mood
meant I was lovable after all.

Rolling Smokes

I boil the kettle while Lucy rolls joints
and explains how her ex
has landed a TV commercial for zits.
No way I'd get back with him now.
Kate's welcome to him.
She laughs and I copy her,
pouring milk into steaming mugs.

I laugh
        not because I see what's funny
but because
I do not want to be alone.

                    I must try harder.

Scabby

The burn itches.
A scab is forming.
I pick at its
crumbly, crusty
edges
until it stings.

Allowed

Marla is sitting on the stairs
in her raincoat.
Hood up,
           mouth down.
What's happening? I ask.

I'm not allowed out.
I mean, is it prison I'm in or what?
Who put up that sign?
I feel like bloody Oscar Wilde
without the hat.
           Or the talent.

I don't know, I say,
glad the sign is there and Marla
knew to stay put.

Why don't we go to the corner store
for some sweets? I suggest,
handing Marla her handbag.

She smiles at the front door,
points at the letter-size printed sign on it.
And I'm taking that down.

IMPORTANT: DO NOT GO OUT ALONE.
CALL PEGGY IF YOU NEED ANYTHING.

We leave the house.
And we leave the sign.

Conkers

Marla stops, stoops,
picks a chestnut from the path.
I love the feel of them.
It's a shame the season ends so quickly,
    isn't it?
Before you know where you are
they wrinkle up and go all wrong.
Like people, I suppose.
    She pockets her find.

I reach down,
    curl my fingers around
    a flat-edged conker nut,
then find another, and another,
collect until my pockets bulge.
I like them too, I admit,
but Marla is already ahead of me
    at the crossing.

    I run to catch up,
to stop her stepping into the road.
She looks surprised to see me at her side.
Hello again, she says.
Now isn't it nice to be together like this?

Stinging Nettles

The conkers fell,
crashing to the ground and shaking off their
    tough-on-the-outside,
    velvety-on-the-inside
    shells.
I begged Kelly-Anne to walk with me to the park
so I could gather a bagful
and take them to school
to boast about I-don't-know-what.

Dad stood up from the couch. *I'll come for some air.*

Kelly-Anne beamed;
    it was before
he started treating her really badly,
and I was probably pleased too.
Dad never went anywhere with us
unless it was somehow about him—
    a trip to Home Depot for paint
    or the Chinese place for dinner.

It was drizzling at Downhills Park.
You could spot the chestnut trees easily,
brown-leaved against a sky of still greens.

I sprinted.
I foraged.

My bag filled quickly with the
chocolatey-brown globes,
but I was greedy for more
and more
and more,
crawled my way beneath briars to trawl.

I didn't see the stinging nettles,
didn't notice the blanket of them
or that my hands, knees, and legs tingled,
until it was too late,
until my body was covered in their toxins
and I was scratching, scratching,
spotting uncased chestnuts but too sore
to collect them.
Oh, you poor thing, said Kelly-Anne,
kneading my hands with dock leaves.

Dad was grinning.
Even I spotted the nettles.
You're too old to be collecting conkers anyway.

I was eleven.
At twelve
        I didn't bother
collecting conkers come September,
and when I was thirteen I told
anyone who flaunted theirs
how stupid and babyish they were
until they hid their treasure
or threw them away entirely.

Babyish

Dad badgered me to
grow up
hurry up
shut up
stop being a baby
stop whining
stop moaning
act my age
act like an adult
quit the crocodile tears,
as though
being a child was a serious problem
and something I could remedy.

Carol and Lee

I was little when
Dad decided he was in love
with someone called Carol
and invited her to live in our house
                                    with her son.
So Carol and Lee
stayed with Dad and me
for a few months.
At first it was easy.
Carol liked baking.
Lee was quiet.
Then Carol quit with the buns and
took to shouting at Lee until he cried.
He was older than I was—
        eight maybe—
        and hated when I saw him tearful,
        hit me to make me unnotice.
It's your stupid fault, he said.
She didn't want a daughter.
She doesn't like you.

I watched Carol.
It wasn't hard to see that Lee was right.

She never tucked me in at night
or washed my uniform for school.
She scowled at me
and at Dad too sometimes,
until one day they were gone—
        Carol and Lee—
and Dad and I carried on as usual,
pretending no one was missing.
Pretending we were happy alone.

Loss

It wasn't like that when Kelly-Anne dumped us.
We couldn't pretend she had never existed
because we were so charged up on her.

I didn't believe Dad could get meaner, but he did.

It was grief. I get it.
Like how he never got over Mum.

But was it my fault everyone left?
Can Dad's life really have been all my fault?

Sometimes I Forget

Sometimes I forget I was born to an actual mother
with wide arms and a smile.

Sometimes I feel so grimy
I can't believe anyone ever longed for me enough
to tear herself open
to give me breath.

Sometimes I think all I am is how he made me
feel:
      sunken,
      small,

        better off
               gone.

Sometimes Kelly-Anne told me I wasn't to blame.
She said, *Shit happens, Allie,*
but not much else
because we didn't talk about Mum in my house,
as though exposing the past
could make stuff
worse than it was.

We nudged the truth out of the way with our elbows
and waded through heavy silence.

Until the noise came.
Which it always did.
A tornado of anger and insults,
a one-man performance that left me in turtlenecks
for a week.

Sometimes I forget I was born to an actual mother
who loved me enough to knit a sweater
the color of orange Fanta,
arms like baby carrots.

But she left too soon and never finished it.

<blockquote>
She left as soon as I arrived.
She left because I arrived.
</blockquote>

A Father Too

Sometimes I forgot my father was the way he was
and I smiled when I saw him,
when he gave me dinner money
or nodded at good grades.
Some Sundays when my father roasted chicken
I'd forget whatever had happened on Saturday night
or think it hadn't been him at all,
that I'd made a mistake in my remembering.
Sometimes I held on to the nice things because the horrible
seemed impossible.
Sometimes I forgot my father was the way he was
and that's why I loved him.

I Did Not Kill My Mother Immediately

It was hours after I arrived that she died.

Mum carried me home in a hospital blanket,
a cocooned caterpillar in her arms,
barely clinging to life.
She opened all the onesies we'd been given
and lay me in a new cot to sleep.
She watched me,
and cooed, amazed by her achievement.

I slept.
Soundly.

But when my eyes opened,
  Mum was gone.
And she never returned,
  though I squealed like a
      banshee.

She was in an ambulance,
or back on a hospital ward,
doctors doing their best to stop her from
      disappearing.

Dad sent in a neighbor to stem the crying.

But when he returned from the hospital the next day,
ashen and alone,
        a wife down, a newborn heavier,
he chose to place every sorrow
in his heart on my head
and looked at me thinking:
                        You did this . . .

Dad never realized that hers was the skin I needed,
the smell and the taste.
Dad never realized that I loved my mother
from the
        inside out,
        before I'd ever known her face,
and that while he might find another wife,

        I would never
                        ever
        get another mother.

Are You My Daughter?

Are you my daughter?
Marla is standing in the hallway,
staring at the wedding band on her fourth finger.
Sometimes I forget, she says.
I'm a gobshite.
I couldn't even tell you what day it is.
Is it Friday?

No, I say. *It's Monday.*

How do you know?

Umm. Because tomorrow is Tuesday.

She rolls her eyes.
I turn on the bathroom light.
And I'm not your daughter.
I'm Toffee.
Do you need anything? I ask.

She blinks slowly,
and rubs her hip.
To sleep. I just need a good old sleep.

It is three o'clock in the afternoon.

Giant Rock Candy

Lucy buys us both a giant red rock candy
from a kiosk on the seafront,
        unwraps hers, and licks the end of it.
That's your sugar fix for the month, I say.

Shh, baby, shh.
She laughs,
                unwraps mine,
pushes the candy
all the way into my mouth
so I am completely gagged.

Do you have a boyfriend? Lucy asks.

I shake my head no.

Yeah, I guessed that.
You totally read as a virgin.

I keep the candy in my mouth
much longer than is necessary.

It stops me from saying the wrong thing—
telling Lucy the ways
in which
I can read her too.

Screaming

Screaming and scratching at the bathroom mirror
with a purple lipstick,
lines and frantic scribbles.
No! No! Not me. Who? NO!
No! Go away! Go AWAY!

I wrap Marla in my arms,
                              drag her onto the landing.
What's wrong?

Her whole body is shivering.
Hands shaking.
Someone was in there.
Someone not me was in there.
An old lady.
Not me.
Get away!
No.
Jesus.
Call Mam and tell her.

No one's here except me, Marla.
I take the lipstick from her hand
and, without knowing why,

154

draw a thick mustache above my top lip.
Was it Madame Croissant?

Her breathing slows. I let go.
You're a silly fecker.

And proud of it, I tell her,
rubbing the mustache with my fingertips.

Who was in there? she whispers.
Who was that woman?
We should go.
She looked shocking.

She's gone, I say.
Shall we dance?
Roger expects us to practice.
We need to be good.
Don't want Moira beating us.

Scrubber.
Moira, I mean.
Not you.
You're dead classy.

Mashed Potato

We are up, moving,
Marla oozing energy,
        sliding left and right,
feet smoothing forward, back,
arms up,
down,
twisting, twirling,
smile so wide
I can see to the back
where she has teeth missing.
I copy her
dancing to "Mashed Potato Time"
by Dee Dee Sharp and her
smile too,
wishing we really were rehearsing for something.

Wishing my life had a purpose.

Slam

I'm taking a pee break
when the front door slams
and heavy footsteps
enter the hallway.
Mum? It's Donal.
Where are you?
Oi, Mum!

Frozen

Donal reprimands Marla like a headmaster
scolding a disobedient student,
and between rebukes
     he sighs,
as though conversation itself
is taxing.
I know you like cheese, Mum,
but it doesn't go in the DVD player.
And what is this?
His voice is like a hedge trimmer—
loud, sharp, dangerous.
It could cut.

     The downstairs bathroom
      is across the hall from the sitting room.
        I crack open the door to see.

Donal is flourishing our feather boa.

     Marla's face is stone.

I've told you a hundred times to take it easy.
Last thing anyone needs is an accident.

I hope you haven't been going out.
He paces the living room,
fishing for mistakes—
lifting knickknacks and jiggling them in her face.

Marla is as still as glass.

    This is none of the Marlas I know.
    This is someone pulled back
        into herself.

                As good as gone.

You're sulking, he says,
prodding her arm with the remote control.
Why are you sulking?
What have I said?
For God's sake, here we go.

    A memory slithers back to me
    and I watch, as frozen as she is.

I'm shattered, Marla mutters.
I've been up late these last nights.

And you don't think I'm tired?
I've been at work all week
and this is my treat.
A mother who forgets who I am half the time.
Place is a pigsty.
What are we paying Peggy for?
Was she even in today?
Not that you'd remember.

I know who you are, Donal, she croaks.

You do?
Brilliant.
      Here's a prize, he says,
and smacks her on the arm
with the remote.

The present and past collide.
      I slide the door shut,
slip onto the floor,
and put my hands over my ears.

Should Have

It is dark when Donal leaves.

In the sitting room
Marla is quiet.

I'm sorry, I say.
*I wanted to stop him
being mean but—*

Who? she says.
You wanted to stop who?

Before I can remind her, she is crying
and mumbling Mary's name
over
and
over
and
over.

Two Hours Later

She looks across at me.
Are you a friend of Mary's?

No, Marla. I'm a friend of yours.

Planning

It is hard not knowing when
people will arrive at Marla's house,
trying to be out as much as I can,
jumping each time the doorbell chimes.

I find her phone
and scroll through
the reminders in her calendar—
      daily, it says "Peggy,"
      weekly, Donal's name appears,
      Mary is nowhere.
And there are other things,
like reminders for medicine
and doctor's visits,
notes about birthdays and
public holidays.

This helps her, I know.
I've seen her check her phone when it pings
and find peace in the written words.

And so I add another.
      "Toffee,"

I type,
        a recurring reminder.

Nothing else.

It should be enough.

Makeup

Marla has old-fashioned compacts
and bronzers too, which I use to
make myself implausibly tanned—
    skin the color of apricots.

I look ridiculous.

Question is:
Do I still look like a scabby virgin?

Homework

Lucy punches a page covered in gray smudges.
Math is such a waste of my life, she groans,
casting the pencil aside.
You look clever. Are you?
Like, help me.
She pushes her books
across the beach-hut table.
My ex-friend used to be good at this crap.
I can't be bothered.

I study the problems.
Nothing hard:
I could finish the page in five minutes
and we could go to the lighthouse,
lie on our backs in reach of the sea's spray.
Shall I teach you how to do it?

No. Just do it. I don't need to know.
She lights up a joint, starts to smoke.

After a few minutes
I slide the exercise book back to her.

You done? How?

I don't know. It's easy.

Lucy leans back, taps her chin with her finger.
Where do you go to school?

Nowhere. I'm homeschooled.

Well, that makes sense.

Why?

Your clothes for a start.
You dress like a wife.
But homeschooled is better actually,
she says with satisfaction.
You wanna earn some cash?

Jobs

Lucy has three jobs lined up
before I leave the beach hut:
 a chemistry project,
 some math,
 a personal statement for a college application.

If I do the work, I get paid,
wouldn't have to scam off Marla anymore,
could stop putting my hand into her purse.
      Lucy gets a cut of course.

Why don't they just do the homework themselves?
They won't learn anything in the long run.

Lucy is confused.
You're not one of those saints, are you?

I think about everything I'm missing from school—
how I might have had a shot at college before
I ran away.
Now I won't even get to do my exams—
stuff I could pass
without much preparation at all.
I'll be poor and end up like Kelly-Anne,
relying on men who make me miserable.

Lucy passes the joint.
I shake my head and instead
help myself to some of her gummy bears.
The little bears are sweet.

You're hiding something, she says.

Hiding

I am hiding my mother, my father,
and my father's women.

I am hiding my old home, my new home,
my old friends, and Marla.

I am hiding my body, my bruises,
my scars, and my burns.

I am hiding my whole history,
                    hoping I will forget it.

I am hiding *everything* from you.

If only I could hide it from myself.

I Tell Lucy

I'm not hiding anything.
Why would you think that?

Shady

As she is locking up the beach hut
Lucy lays her fingers on my shoulder.
I know you've got that thing on your face.
But the makeup looks so trashy.
Like a guidette or something. Just saying.

I nod. *I know.*
And I do.

She nudges me and twinkles a smile
as though we've just had
the deepest conversation
ever.
Your skill is your smarts.

Normals

Being smart wasn't enough to get me noticed
in a school of fifteen hundred.
For that you needed beauty,
had to be someone with even edges and sleek hair.
Or
if not,
a kid with serious psychological problems—
        there were loads of those.

For a while
        Sophie, Jacq, and I called ourselves
        the Normals,
but it was still a way of trying to
        stand out.
'Scuse us, the Normals have arrived, Jacq would say,
pushing through an army of girls with smooth legs,
the types of figures
to make grown men look.

We were even invisible to the grades below,
although sometimes Sophie
shouldered them out of the way
to prove we weren't nothing.

Thing was,

        Sophie and Jacq really were normal.

At home their mums nagged at them.

At school they got detentions.

At the park boys offered them beer.

They let themselves be seen

and didn't care about mistakes along the way.

If you aren't winning, you're learning,

        Jacq said when Sophie

failed a French test, and they high-fived

before heading into 7-Eleven

for sandwiches.

The Normals was a perfect description for them.

        My friends.

And even though it didn't quite fit me—

        smart and secretive—

they let me along for the ride.

Until finally the ride ended.

The Beginning of Burns

Jacq and Sophie didn't really have a choice.

Jacq said, *Why can't we come in though?*
Sophie said, *You're being pretty bitchy.*
Jacq said, *We got an Uber, Al. Cost us seven quid.*
Sophie said, *I don't think she cares what we did.*

I said, *I'm a bit busy. Can I call you later?*

Jacq said, *What are you doing?*
Sophie said, *A guy probably.*
Jacq said, *It's not Peter, is it?*
Sophie said, *I bet it is. She totally likes him.*

I said, *Please go away.*

Jacq said, *What?*
Sophie said, *You what?*

I said, *Just fuck off, all right,*
and slammed the door.

Inside Dad was asleep.
I went to the bathroom
and found alcohol to clean the cigarette burn.

It was such a small thing
on the back of my hand.
A tiny blistering circle.

Nothing awful
compared to what he'd done before.

But with Kelly-Anne gone he was crueler.
This was the beginning of something new.
The beginning of burns.

Funny Thing Is

Getting a small circular burn
on the back of my hand
wasn't as bad as the week before
when I swore—
    Shit!—
and he heard,
and marched me to the bathroom,
made me brush my teeth
with honeysuckle hand soap
until it foamed up
and filled my whole mouth
with sour froth.

Hot Bread

I'd like some . . . Marla hesitates.
Bread.

I stand.

       I bought bread with seeds earlier.
       Got the baker to slice it
       even though it was still slightly warm.

I want it hot, she says.

It won't be hot now.

Make it hot. She is annoyed.
She tears at the skin on her arm.
In the thing. I want it crunchy.
Put it in the thing that makes it baked.
Not baked. It's already baked.
Grilled.
Oh, I can do it!
You're absolutely useless.
She tries to get to her feet but is too low
down in the sofa to jump up easily.
She reaches for a cushion
and screams into it.

I let her,
      and when she is done
I say,
      You mean toast, Marla?

She plays with a tassel
on the corner of the throw pillow.
I want some toast.
She sighs.
Toast. Yes. Please.

Out There

Marla's phone pings.
She startles, reads the screen, and smiles.

A reminder,
             or a message maybe,
someone remembering she exists.

That must be nice.
To know that   out there
somewhere
she is alive in another person's mind.

With no phone I can't know
whether anyone is thinking of me or not,
whether Dad and Kelly-Anne
have inundated me with desperate messages.

But it would be nice.
To know that   out there
somewhere
I am being remembered.

One Thing

Lucy is sitting on the beach next to another girl.
    This is my friend Mindy.
The girl nods,
      gawking into her phone
      and grinning.
      Someone else is behind them,
      standing over a mountain bike,
         a cigarette limp between her lips.
      And that's Jan.
      Lucy points
         but doesn't turn.
      She's sort of retro.
She must mean the cigarette but I don't know.

Lucy gives me twelve quid
for the completed homework plus
two more math assignments.

Can you translate French? Jan asks.
She sucks on the cigarette
like someone who hasn't been
smoking very long—
a quick pull,
hardly inhaling.

I can do most subjects.
It sounds arrogant
but all I mean is that
studying is the one thing I can do.
One thing out of a hundred failures.

My dad is being a real pain
and it's parents' evening next week.
Jan speaks to my burn.
I flick my hair to cover it.
I've tried Google Translate but it's pointless.
I need to write a description of my family.
You can make it up.

All right.

Another senior needs a personal statement
for UCAS, Lucy adds.
I can give you bullet points.

I'm about to smile gratefully but say instead,
their college application will cost extra.
The last one took forever.

Lucy grins. *Of course.*
I mean,
        time is money.
Right?

182

Sexier

I am sitting at the kitchen table translating for cash.
Was there homework? Marla asks.
I thought we were on midterm break.
What's that you're doing?
God, Sister Gwendoline never gives up.
She peers over my shoulder.
      Oh. French. Sexy.
Monsieur Hogan est plus sexy que
Monsieur Taylor,
      tu ne penses pas?
      Oui? Oui?

Oui! I say,
handing over some loose-leaf paper
      and putting her to work.

It's not taking advantage.
Not really: it's good for her brain.

Not Lost

It is on the news.
The story of a girl aged fifteen
who went missing five days ago.

She is not me.

Her name is Faye Paterson.
Her parents are frantic.
Her mother is speaking in gray tones.
Her father is gray.

She is not me.

Faye was last seen outside a café,
wearing jeans and a hoodie,
holding her phone close,
waiting for friends.

She is not me.

Faye is MISSING,
and police would like help finding her.
Everyone is worried.

But who is looking for me?
I am missing
too.

And yet
I am lost to nobody.

Trick or Treat

Marla knows it is Halloween
and demands we trick-or-treat
for sweets
along the street
like little children.

It is beyond embarrassing,
      the two of us in heavy eye shadow
      and not much else spooky
      apart from lip liner
      like blood
      trickling down
      our chins.

But we fill a basket with gum
and chocolate
and lollipops
and chewy candy,

and once we are sitting to watch the news,
the humiliation,
the snickers, stares, and furrowed brows
somehow seem worth it.

Whatever

Lucy pays me for more homework,
        two essays and a science experiment.
        I hold the money in my hand and say,
I lost my phone.
I don't suppose you know anyone
selling theirs?

She looks at me with a bored expression.
Oh, I thought you didn't have one
'cause your parents are hippies or whatever.
Yeah, I've got an old iPhone you can have.

I'd pay, I say.

Whatever. She waves me away.
I'll have a look later.

Fireworks

Banging and cracking.
Darkness filled with
the dust of gunpowder.
Marla hides beneath her
duvet like a kitten.

Who knows what lurks
in the minds of others—
the grief they have gobbled up
and stashed away?

Phobia

Dad had a phobia of cats.
He jumped behind me whenever he saw one,
thumped on the windows
if a stray pissed in our yard.
When it was me, Dad, and a cat,
I wasn't scared.

When it was me, Dad, and a cat,
I was safe.

Before Kelly-Anne

Dad liked showing me off,
boasting about how responsible I was:
Al's been washing her own hair since she was six,
he'd tell his girlfriends,
like this was something to puff up with pride over
and not a shitting disgrace.

The women would blink, shrug, smile,
until Dad took them upstairs,
where they made sounds like
he was hurting them,
      which is what I thought was happening,
until I realized
      they liked it.
      The hurting he was doing.

I'd play outside,
lie looking up at the sky.

Some women stayed a few days,
Tanya weeks,
Carol a whole six months,
but no one stayed as long as Kelly-Anne.

No one else was prepared
to put up with the pain
that came with loving him.

Apart from me.

The Missing Girl

Faye Paterson is found alive in Newcastle,
working behind a bar for her older boyfriend.
He called the police himself after the media storm.
I didn't abduct her.
Didn't know she was underage.
I promise. I promise. I promise.

No one expected it.
Everyone suspected her father
after his silence in the interviews—
his quiet tears.
He was a man with stubble
and a shirt buttoned up too tight
to be trusted.

They'd found blood
and were digging up her backyard.

Marla says,
She isn't dead then?
That girl.

No, she was pouring pints.
She ran away.

Is that what happened to my Mary?
Is that where she is?

I don't know to be honest.

Marla is silent for many minutes.
And you. Why did you run away?

When to Leave

I knew before the ruby ring got cold
     on the hall table
that I should've left with Kelly-Anne.
I should have chased her down Dongola Road
with my shoelaces undone.

I should've left sooner than I did.

Kelly-Anne stayed too long.

But people hang around at football games
when their teams are losing
and sure to be beaten.
They wait until the end of movies they hate
instead of walking out
and getting their money back.

People stay all the time—
                      endure boredom
                      and sorrow.

I suppose when it's too painful to stay,
that is when we leave.

Because it isn't true that love hurts.
It doesn't always.

Love doesn't always have to hurt.

Distrust

Sitting on the rocks by the lighthouse,
the occasional cool spray of ocean on her face,
Lucy says,
> *Are you homeless?*

No. I live up Poughill way.

Cool.
So we should go to your place.
Nothing about her voice believes me,
though I'm not sure how I gave anything away.
> Is this how Marla feels whenever she speaks?
> Like the world is sneering?

A seagull lands a few yards from us,
a half loaf of bread in its beak.
We can go whenever you like.
Right now if you want.

The seagull squawks.

I'm meeting someone. Can't.
She throws a stone at the seagull.
Birds are idiots.

Slippers

I have commandeered Marla's slippers.
She had four pairs
lined up neatly under the stairs—
ratty but tidy.

So I've taken the brown ones
with the fur inside
and wear them in the house
instead of my sneakers.

At home Dad didn't like
slippers
or pajamas
or anything that looked like
bedtime
wandering around during the day.

He said it made people look unemployed.

Marla points at my feet.
Aren't those mine?

The hairy ankles?
No. They're mine.
You can touch them if you like.

The slippers, she says,
      grinning at the joke.

Oh yes, they're yours.

Well, I hope your feet are clean.
Not that mine were last time I wore them!

Who Did That to Your Face?

She asks.

No One Did Anything to Me

I tell her.

Memories

If I could forget what he did
   I could go home.
We could be like nothing awful
ever happened.

I wouldn't even need to forgive him.

But my memory,
like an animal hungry to be fed,
hangs on
        with gritted teeth
to
        everything.

Witchy

I had a pet rabbit, Marla says.
I can't remember its name for the life of me.
I wish I could remember its name.
A white fluff ball.

Fluffy? I suggest.

You're a witch! she shouts.
Fluffy! Yes, Fluffy, that was it.
You're a witch, you know that?

If I were a witch I'd do more
than guess animal names.
I'd cast spells on the whole world.
And on myself.

Sure, what would you change about yourself?
Aren't you good enough as you are?

I have no reply.
It might be the kindest thing
anyone has ever said to me.

I Sort of Do, Yeah

The turnaround of homework is quick.
Lucy lines up more and more customers,
everyone pleased with what I've produced—
someone even asking if I can put together a
poetry portfolio.
What about their exams? I ask.
What's the point of all this if they fail in the end?

Lucy snaps her chewing gum,
hands me eighteen pounds and fifty pence
        plus some history-homework guidelines.
I don't really care about their lives. Do you?

Drug Store

I buy a Snickers, Bounty, Kit Kat, and Twix.
I buy YoCrunch yogurts and salted butter.
I buy two microwaveable pasta meals,
an iceberg lettuce, and a loaf of brown bread.
I buy toilet paper, tampons, soap.
I buy what I have stolen from Marla
and what I now need—
        what can be paid for with cash anyway.

Alone

The whole house is dark.
The back door is locked.

I collect the spare key from
beneath the stone leprechaun
on the patio
and let myself in,
stare at my murky reflection
in the kitchen clock face.

Hello?
      Nothing answers.

      I am unsure what to do,
      wondering where Marla could be,
      if she's with anybody,
      whether there's been an emergency.

I take the stairs two at a time,
march into Marla's bedroom.

Her dressing table is littered with
      little perfume bottles—
brands I don't know,

the liquid inside piss-yellow
and smelling of antiseptic.
And she has talc too,
    like flour,
       with a pink puff on top.
I sniff and realize this is Marla's smell—
    powdery petals.

In her black-lacquered jewelry box
are cheap chains and bracelets
clenched together in forever tangles.

I run my fingers along a row of rings,
    pausing at a ruby,
then clutch the pendant
pressed against my own chest,
a silver chalice Mum was given
for her First Holy Communion—
    the only token Dad was prepared to share.

I'm home! Marla calls out.
I step onto the landing, ready to reply,
ready to be annoyed with her for disappearing,
when I see Peggy pulling Marla out of a coat.
They murmur flatly.

Toffee? Marla calls again. *I'm home.*

I press my back against the wood-chip wallpaper.

And you won twenty pounds,
      Peggy says.
Maybe tell Toffee about it tomorrow.
She doesn't seem to be here.
I'd love to meet her actually.

She's here now, Marla says.

The carpet beneath my feet seems to murmur
and the air around me is heavy.
I hold my breath,
pray that Peggy doesn't notice my stupid parka,
which can have nothing to do with an old woman.

Maybe she's asleep, Marla suggests.
Lazy scut.

Peggy calls out herself: *Toffee!*
But again,
      this is pantomime, placation,
and I want to step forward,
stand at the top of the stairs and say,

She isn't nuts; I'm real.
Look at me. I am standing right here
and I am alive.

And then the thought strikes me that
perhaps
I'm not.

Perhaps
I am a figment
                    of Marla's imagination
                    after all.

I touch the chalice against my skin.

Maybe I'm just like my mother—
mostly dead
and only barely
clinging on
in other people's
memories.

Old Enough

On March 7 every year,
the anniversary of Mum's death,
we took time to remember her.

We went to the graveyard,
        laid roses,
and told her the good bits from
our lives—
        when we could think of them.

Kelly-Anne left us to it.
Not that we did very much.

And one year
when we got home
Dad rummaged around in his room, then came
        down
with the silver chalice pendant
on a chain.
This was hers, he said.
You're old enough to wear it
and take care of it, I suppose.
He held it a moment before handing it over.

Thanks, I said.

He shrugged.
Yeah. Well.
I'm not into all that religious bullshit
anyway.

Smash

Once Peggy is out the door
I dash downstairs.
Marla is reading a magazine
upside down,
her head at an angle.

Hey.
She reaches into the pocket of her skirt,
pulling out two tens.
I won at bingo! she announces,
bobbing in her chair.
Three fat ladies.
Or two.
Fat ladies for the win!
I love a fat lady.
And fat men.
I'd love any man though.

Save it, I suggest.

Or spend it on gin. She grins.
The liquor store is still open.
I saw the lights from the car.

I haven't had alcohol
since Sophie stole
a bottle of Bacardi
from her aunt's dresser.
I hated the taste,
liked the feeling of being only half-present.

I'll get our coats, I say.

Gin Is Tonic

Marla snickers and pours,
dribbling in the gin
then topping off with tonic.

      The drink fizzes
      in delight.

Ice, she says.
See if there's any in the . . . the . . .

        Freezer, I finish,
           and go on a hunt.

I crack cubes into the glasses,
booze splashing back at me.

Marla looks as nervous as I feel
with the rim to her lips,
like someone who's never touched a drop
despite mixing them up
like an expert,
        the recall
        in her hands
        if not in her head.

We are being bad, she says.

I swig. *We are.*
We are being a bit bad.

She touches my hand.
If Mam finds out she'll
take a leather shoe to me.
If Daddy finds out he'll peel me alive.

No one will ever know, Marla.
Clinking glasses,
we guzzle.

Single Ladies

Marla and I are giggling,
clinging to each other,
swaying, spinning to
Beyoncé singing out
from the radio's tinny speakers.

Now like this! Like this! I tell her.
I hold one hand aloft and twirl it
like any single lady would,
and Marla copies the choreography—
       hands in the air,
       hands on hips,
       fists punching forward,
       hair flicked back.

It's too quick. She is breathless,
stepping up to the mantelpiece and
pouring more gin into her glass.
Show me again!

I fall to my knees laughing.
Her Beyoncé is appalling.

But she is beautiful.

Hangover

I comb through
Marla's medicine cabinet for painkillers
before crawling back into bed with my sore head,
a pint of tap water,
a sack of self-loathing,
and a promise to myself
never
to drink
again.

Any Jewels?

Jan is with Lucy at the beach hut.

It feels rude to say no
to the slim bottles of beer on offer,
so by 7:00 p.m.
      I am staggering home,
      totally smashed,
      Lucy managing both to keep me up
                    and use me
                    as a crutch.
      Jan snickers
      behind her hand
      about *lightweights*,
      like she isn't wasted herself.

At Marla's back gate
Lucy says, seeming surprised,
      It's a house.

My stepmum's mum,
      my stepmum's mum's,
I slur, blinking slowly.

      Lucy says,
      Has she got any booze?

Has she got any jewels?
My nana's loaded, Jan adds.

Tomorrow, I say.
       I'd have to ask first.

Lucy leans in and hugs me,
her grasp heavy, hard, unexpected.

      I hiccup and hold on to
          the gatepost
          to stop myself from
          sliding
          onto
          the ground.

Come over to my place on Saturday.
Hopefully my parents won't be home.
I can give you that phone, Lucy says.

      I can't stay to say thank you.
      I might be sick.

And then I am.

In Marla's grass,
    while Lucy stumbles away,
    trailed by her friend,
    their laughter
    hollow.

Have You Seen?

Have you seen my pen?
Marla shuffles in her chair,
grumbles,
disturbs the cushion and crossword on her lap.
     I had it only a second ago.

I am slumped,
hungover again,
but jump up, head spinning,
and search for the pen myself,
lifting magazines,
     rifling through a bowl of keys
          and junk.
What are you doing? Marla asks.

Looking for your pen.

Why?
You didn't take it.
Did you?

Where's the Remote?

When Dad asked a question like
    Where's the remote?
what he meant was:
    Find the remote.

Or when he said,
    What's for dinner?
what he meant was:
    I am hungry. Feed me.

Dad's questions were never queries—
    they were demands
    and judgments,
    weapons to make me nervous.

Dad's problems were mine.

His discontent
    something I did my best
        to fix.

The White House

It's the white house,
    Lucy had said,
which I took to mean
    it's
    a
    white house.

But no.

Her house is, as she said,
    the
    white house,
the only one on the street,
a street of three homes differentiated
by color—white, yellow, brown—
each topped with glass and jutting out
over the ocean like coastal guardians.

I press the bell and, as if I've cast a spell,
a woman in gardening gloves appears at my side
carrying two empty wine bottles.
Well, hello there, she says.
Before I can reply,

Lucy opens the door and
pulls me into the house.

Her mother follows.
Her hair is sprayed stiff;
        her face doesn't move.
Would you like anything to eat, darling?
        I can ask Stacey to fix you something.
        I'm going out soonish.

I produce a bar of milk chocolate
and hand it to her mum,
who checks the purple wrapping, back and front,
like it's a quiz.
Thanks for having me, I say,
ashamed I thought
such a small thing could be a gift.

Oh, that's incredibly thoughtful of you.
How extraordinary.
Lucy, look at this?
She forgot my birthday last month.
Don't even ask me what happens on Mother's Day!
Little Miss Forgetful.
I'd rather believe that than think my child doesn't care.

Lucy groans, drags me upstairs.
Jesus. Sorry about that.
Thought she'd be at a flaxseed convention
or something.

I don't speak,
focus on keeping my mouth closed
and not going too goggle-eyed at her room:
> at the wide-screen TV
> next to the PC
> next to the laptop
> next to the double wardrobe
> next to the double bed
> next to the acoustic guitar
> next to the drum set
> next to the bathroom.

You've got your own flat.

Lucy scans the room unimpressed.
It stinks in here.
I had the dog with me.
Mum won't put her down.
Should we work first or watch Netflix?

Lucy hands me an essay,
a teacher's red marks in the margins.

Got this back yesterday.
Need to fix it.
Will you help?

I hadn't expected to work.
I shrug. *Sure.*

For the rest of the afternoon
I sit at her desk overlooking the ocean
and type into the laptop
while Lucy lolls on her bed
watching movies,
occasionally passing me
a sandwich or piece of fruit delivered to the room
by a housekeeper.

At six o'clock her dad arrives home.
Lucy takes me down to say hello.
He is wearing a raincoat
though it's sunny outside.
I've been sailing.
Lovely day for it.

I try to look interested but I've got no idea
what sailing means—
        was he in a boat as big as a dinghy

or something more like a yacht?
Did he fish?
Is he a captain?
I think of Sophie and Jacq—
what they'd say if they could see this place,
meet this family—
how they'd run out of *shitting hells*
and *oh my god*s.
    They'd swipe stuff for sure.
You're welcome to stay for supper,
    her dad assures me,
pronouncing it *sup-pah*
then heading away from the kitchen,
where a woman is dutifully chopping.

I better get back.
Maybe Marla won't have noticed the time
or that I'm missing,
but I don't want to eat with these people watching,
trying to keep my knife, napkin, glass
in the right places.

In the hallway
Lucy hands me more homework.
Need it back by Tuesday.
You're getting slower, you know?

This stuff's not for me obviously.
Oh and here. Take this.
　　　She pulls an iPhone from her back pocket.

Are you sure?

Part payment for the homework, she says.
You'll need to get it unlocked.

Behind her
on the table
is the bar of Cadbury chocolate.

I reach one hand forward and
　　　slip it into my coat.

Marla's Tiny Terraced House

Marla's house must have been painted white
      some time ago,
though now it looks gray
from weather-wear
and lack of care.
    She is sitting on the back step,
staring at a pack of cigarettes.
Are these yours? she asks.
I shake my head.
Maybe they're Mary's.
Find a lighter.
Or you could use the grill.

I pull out the chocolate bar.
How about this instead?

Is it all for me?

You have to share, I scold.

Fair enough.
She swaps cigarettes for chocolate,
yumming so loudly
you'd think we were eating

in a five-star restaurant.
I'm glad you got milk chocolate.
The dark stuff tastes like cough syrup.

Yeah. Why would anyone eat it?

Trying to be posh.

Can you be a chocolate snob?

You can be any sort of snob at all.
That's how the la-di-das sniff us out—
by noticing what we wear and buy and eat and everything.
A snob would know you didn't belong in two seconds flat,
she says.

I suppose so.
I think of how Lucy could tell
by studying my shoelaces
that I don't belong in her world.

Marla has chocolate in her eyebrow.
I rub it away with my thumb.
Shall we have supper?

She looks up at the sky.
But it isn't bedtime.
That wouldn't make sense.

No, I say. *No, it wouldn't.*

So we have TV dinners instead.
Like common people.

Meeting Marla

Marla is kneeling on the sitting-room carpet,
    tearing pages from
a paperback.

I'm home. This is Lucy, I say.

She doesn't look up.
You're not Peggy.
She holds the book aloft.
Is this mine?
Who's that?

Everything's yours, I explain,
wishing she was sane today.
This is Lucy.
Should I make tea?

Coffee, she snaps.
And a sandwich. Did you pick up ham?
When's dinner?
I've been hungry since last Sunday.
Did you know Michael Jackson died?
They just said it on the telly.
I loved his song about killers.

Thriller.

Thriller. *That's the one.*
With all the zombies.
That was great.
Who else is dead that I should know about?

We have ham, I say.

Lucy follows me to the kitchen,
slumps at the table.
What's wrong with her?
She helps herself to an apple from the
       fruit bowl.

She forgets stuff, I say. *It's dementia.*

Old people are nuts! She laughs.

Something in my stomach knots.

We ascend the stairs on tiptoe,
       avoiding the final one, which creaks.
Lucy strolls to the window.
So Marla's your great-aunt?

She hadn't been listening,
    which I suppose,
        when it comes
  to stuff about Marla,
isn't a bad thing.

No, she's my sort-of-stepmum's mother, I say,
    repeating the lie
and able to tell something about how I arrived
and found Kelly-Anne gone—
replacing Marla for the man in the soccer shirt,
telling Lucy some of the truth for once.

I want to get away sometimes.
Mum is a total migraine.
She paws at a porcelain ornament on the dressing
table—
    an angel with a harp—
    turns it upside down to read the bottom,
    like she knows what the markings mean.

Then she opens a drawer,
        the top one, stuffed with patchwork quilts,
rummages a bit,
closes it again.

What are you looking for?

Dunno. I better go actually.
I've got a drum lesson at seven.

The clock on the wall ticks loudly.
It is five o'clock.

Don't you want to have your coffee?
I'll make it and you can chat with Marla.

Jan's expecting me.
I better go, she repeats,
        and she does.

People

What is it they want anyway?

Bath Time

Allison! Kelly-Anne called out.
She was in the bathroom,
standing over a steaming tub of bubbles.
I stood at the door,
> thought she was going to ask me where we
> kept the conditioner.
Get in, she said.

I stayed by the door,
> wore my best stepdaughter face.
>> It was my house.
>> She wasn't my mum.
Anyway I was ten:
> too old to be told when to wash.
And she'd been living with us three days:
> too soon to be ordering me around.

Your hair's filthy, she said flatly.
You can't go to school like that.
Get in.

The TV blared downstairs,
> Dad watching *SportsCenter*,

Kelly-Anne and me keeping away after
Spurs got knocked out of the FA Cup.

I'll have a shower tomorrow, I lied,
and stomped to my room,
slamming the door
just enough to show her who was boss,
              not so much to make Dad mad.

She knocked.
      Allison, you need a wash.

My hands were covered in ink stains.
I'd been wearing the same socks for days.
      How had I not noticed?
Why had Dad never said anything?
      I sniffed my armpit.
Shame, like slime, filled my whole body.
I began to cry.
I don't want a bath, I shouted.

Kelly-Anne charged into my room,
put one hand on her hip,
with the other pointed to the bathroom.
Go and have a bath this minute, she hissed.

I narrowed my eyes,
felt like spitting at her.

Instead I had a bath.
                    It was lovely.
                    It was long.

And afterward,
        with an expression like concrete,
I let Kelly-Anne blow-dry my hair straight,
faking being furious,
secretly hoping,
even then,
that Dad would drop dead
and leave the two of us to it
forever.

Unlocked

I get the iPhone unlocked
and buy a SIM card so I have a number again,
    a new one,
        making me a real person in the world.

But I don't bother logging in to any of my apps.
I don't try to make contact with
my old life.

For some reason.

Reading the Meter

He's wearing a white T-shirt
rolled up to the shoulder so his biceps bulge,
blue jeans low on his hips.
Just gotta read the meter, guys.
He rummages under the stairs,
giving us a view from the back.
He whistles, hums,
clears his throat of a smoky cough.

Marla elbows me,
      stares at the poor man's ass
      like she's never seen a human being before.
I'd take some of that, she says
far too loudly
and I snort into my hand.

The guy, no more than thirty,
turns and holds up an
               electronic gadget.
Right, all done. I'll get out of your hair.

He hooks both thumbs into his pockets
and looks down at Marla's bare feet,

the toenails painted blue
by me
last night
after I'd done my own
and she demanded I do hers too.
I didn't want to, of course—
get so close to an old lady's gnarly feet.
But I did it anyway.
They were bony, featherlight—
like holding a bird.

No rush now at all, Marla says.
I'll fix you a drink.
Unless you'd like to take me out and buy one.
I like a fruity cocktail.
What about you?
Shall we go for a quick one?
A drink, I mean!

The meter reader rubs one thick eyebrow.
Not sure my missus would like that.

Marla creeps toward him—
takes his hands.
Well, I won't tell her if you don't.

Pneumatic

The meter reader's name is Martin.
He's twenty-six,
lives with his wife and their new baby.
So he stops with us
for an hour rather than going home to
     all that crying—
     and that's just the wife. He laughs
                but it is thin.

Marla slices lemons.
I find tumblers.
We have gin on the patio in our coats,
listening to a far-off pneumatic drill
working very hard to split something in two.

You promise not to tell anyone?
     Martin asks.

I won't say a word, I promise.

And me neither, Marla says,
     eyeing Martin
     in a way that tells me she's already
     completely forgotten who he is.

Can I Owe You?

Lucy hands me another pile of homework.
She seems miles away.
Everything okay? I ask.

She looks over one shoulder,
then the other,
bends down
to pet the dog.
Yeah, fine. Just busy, you know?
I watch while she counts out what she owes me
from the last set of work.
I have five fifty. Can I owe you the rest?
I'm good for it.

It's okay. You gave me the phone.
What was that worth?

Oh yeah. The phone.
I guess we're square then.
You might even owe me.
She grins and pockets the money.

I planned on ordering pizza tonight
with loads of ham for Marla,

maybe Ben & Jerry's for dessert.
Exactly, I say casually,
thinking of her white house,
en suite bathroom,
the suppers.

Do you wanna take a cliff walk? I ask.
We keep meaning to do it,
joke a lot about jumping.

Not today.
Tomorrow maybe.
   She nods to the pile of work.
You're so smart.
Not cool or funny or anything.
But really smart.

Cupcakes

Marla's made cupcakes with white icing,
all laid out on a wire rack,
ready for a pot of tea
and some company.
They smell delicious, I tell her,
and she beams like I've given her
a sticker.

But when we sit down to eat
and Marla bites into the first cake,
her face clouds.

I try one too.
And no.

They are salty when they should be sweet,
though I swallow down my mouthful
instead of spitting it onto the plate.

I am useless, she says.
Feckin' useless. Useless.
I can't even bake a bun.
Seven-year-olds can bake buns.
She hits her own arm.

Her shoulder.
Her face.

I sit very still,
wondering when her hand will reach me.
Not daring to speak,
        an eye on the back door.
I could be out in five seconds.
Stupid, she says.
Stupid,
stupid,
stupid.

And she is right.
I was stupid to
start feeling safe here.
She's not with it.
She could strike out at any moment.

You left out the sugar, that's all, I say.

Yes, I missed the sugar.
I'm not a total gobshite.
I know what I did.
She grinds her teeth,
squints at me for a second.

Have I made this happen?
Have I made her feel this way?

She bangs the table,
hits her arm again.
Stupid, Marla.
Stupid buns.
How did I get so old?
Look at the state of me.

I exhale.
　　She is angry with herself,
　　with her brain,
the strain of her disease.
Marla isn't mad with me at all.

On the countertop are the other ingredients
along with a dusting of flour.
She's left the oven on.

I search for the sugar.
Could you teach me to make them?

She turns away. *Don't get on my nerves.*
A cack-handed blind hedgehog could make them.

I find a tea towel,
      turn it into a blindfold.
Let's test that theory.

You're not a right thing.
You're really not a right thing.
I stretch out my arms toward her like a zombie.
I hear her giggle.
Come here and let me tie that thing tighter.

And so we bake.
Me in a blindfold,
      Marla in charge.

And the buns come out okay.

In the end.

Chats Over Tea and Cupcakes

I haven't heard from Rob Clancy in ages,
                    Marla says.
Did he knock the door there at all?
'Cause I'm sure I heard the door?
Did he knock the door there
when I was in the bathroom?
God, I have an awful stomach on me today.
Have I had prawns?

I shake my head.
No Rob Clancy's come knocking.
We had a Martin recently.
Gin on the patio?

He's probably gallivanting with
that brother of his. Layabouts, both of them.
You'd think they'd get proper jobs instead of
living at home with their mother, who's got enough
to be doing without feeding their blathering face-holes.
Did the brother try to ride you?
Rob Clancy's tried to ride me loads
and I've always said, "Take a hike, Robert Clancy.
I'm not interested in someone with less
ambition than a potato."

I'm not lying.
Rob Clancy wouldn't get out of bed if his house
was on fire.

> *If his bed was on fire, more like.*
> *If his arse, even.*

I'd like to test it by setting his sheets alight.
He had a paper route. Maybe he still does.
They gave him a block of flats
but he wouldn't climb the stairs and didn't he
dump the deliveries in the hall, the useless slug.
You'd think he doesn't have a good pair of legs on him.
But he does.
A great pair of pins.
Nice backside too. Peachy.
Is he nineteen now? He must be.
Old enough not to be a messer.
If he does come knocking, you're having the brother.
He isn't as gorgeous
but he'd pedal a bike for you.
Rob's as lazy as a dog in the summer.
If there was work in his bed
he'd sleep on the floor.
What's the brother called?
Roger.

> *No, not Roger. That's someone else.*

It's Richard.
       Rich and Rob.
That's it.
       Rich and Rob Clancy.
Messers.
Rob's the peachy one.
Rich is missing part of his thumb.
He worked for a butcher and
sliced it off along with some corned beef.
God, I never liked corned beef.
Who'd eat it?
Makes me think of the war.
Makes me think of Mam.
Is Mam not home yet?
Where's she at, at all?
Did she say you could stay over?
I never asked her. I should ask her.
But you're taking the brother.
Deal? Put your hand out there and shake on it.

I'm not taking the brother,
I say.
I'm taking no one.

Marla startles.
You've already got someone.

Is he lovely? I bet he is. Is he lovely?
    Mary's lovely.
    Donal's a scut.
Tell me.
        Have you got a boyfriend?
Sure, you could make anyone love you.
Some people are like that.

You Could Make Anyone Love You

Some people
are like
that.

Valentine's Day

Kelly-Anne and I made a cake from scratch,
Victoria sponge smothered in pink icing
and white sprinkles.

Dad didn't know how to behave
when he got in from work,
when we both kissed him and
gave him homemade cards.

He ate the cake quietly,
unable to look up.
Thank you, he finally muttered.
*But I feel bad 'cause I didn't
do anything special.*

*You don't believe in Valentine's Day, Dad,
that's okay,* I said.

Kelly-Anne nodded, stroked the back of his hand.

He stood up from the table roughly.
*And what does that say about me?
Tell me what it says about a person*

when he can't even buy a box of chocolates
for Valentine's Day.

He cried then.
The first time I'd ever seen it happen,
and Kelly-Anne hugged him until he stopped.

Finally, we knew, he loved us.

Romeo and Juliet

When I was eleven, Mrs. Rufus took the class to see
an amateur performance of *Romeo and Juliet*.
We had studied it. Performed scenes
using swords and headdresses.

The seats were red velvet.
I was on the end of a row next to Jason Clean.
       Weirdly, he smelled of disinfectant,
       carried hand sanitizer on a key ring.
       Everyone called him Spring Clean,
       which wasn't as mean as it could get.
       One girl in the class was called Ugly—
           simple as that, Ugly, no explanation
           needed.

Jason held my hand after the intermission.
I didn't snatch it away
even though his fingers were sweaty
and I was trying to eat a bag of sweets.

He whispered, *Want to kiss on the bus?*

I said, *Sure, yeah, okay, fine.*
       But I was worried.

I'd already promised to sit
with Sophie on the way home
and listen to music, an earbud each.

I had to pass her a note along the row
        to explain I'd agreed to kiss Spring Clean
    and would have to disappoint her,
                disappoint myself.

It was a shame.
I rarely got a chance to listen to music on a phone
and Spring Clean didn't even kiss me in the end.
He was too busy puking into a paper bag
and saying, *sorry-sorry-sorry.*

    But that was love,
    I guessed.

    Love was sacrifice:
    rarely simple,
            rarely even what we wanted.

What I Wanted

Kelly-Anne was the first person who made me
believe love could be easy.

But in the end it was hard
         even with her.

Because she left
and I let her.

Before Bed

Would you call me a blond?
Marla fingers the frizzy ends
of her gray hair.

I'll call you anything you like.

Just don't call me too early in the morning!
She giggles,
        and though I've heard this joke
ten times already from her,
I laugh too,
then stand behind her chair
and begin to give her a French braid,
pulling the short ends in,
smoothing them into place.
You always have gorgeous hair, she says.
She can't mean me,
        my stringy strands
hiding my face.
She must be thinking of Toffee,
tresses to her hips,
        held back
from her forehead with a wide hairband.

I haven't got gorgeous anything, I whisper.

Marla turns angrily,
ruining the braid I'm forced to release.
Do you know your trouble?
You don't half talk a load of old shite.

Behind the Butcher's

The trash cans stink of old meat.
The ground is covered in blood and sawdust.
Lucy and Jan are rolling a joint
and talking fast.
> *And he's, like, "Whatever."*
> *He said "Whatever," like, just like that?*
> *Yeah, I know.*
> *You've gotta ghost him.*
> *Nah, not worth it.*

I don't ask what they're talking about.
I take a drag on the joint
when it comes to me.
Can anyone smell maggots? I ask,
> in case neither of them
has noticed.

Lucy jumps away from the trash.
Eww. You're right.
Let's go to your place instead.

Jan says, *I've got swimming practice, yeah.*

I say, *Yeah, better not.*

Lucy elbows me hard.
Ugh. You're such a pain.

It doesn't feel sore.
It doesn't feel good.
But at least I know I'm alive.
At least when Lucy is around
I know for sure I am not a figment
of someone else's imagination.

I am real.

Darkness

Some people are afraid of the dark.

I am not.

In the daytime I am too scared
to tell a truth of any shape
in case someone looks at me while I am speaking,
notices something crappy,
something they'd rather not see.

But at night,

in the shadows,

without the distractions of the day,
the blinding light,
everything is so much easier.

Usually.

Betrayal

Lucy grins
     like an absurd bandit,
with a flat, empty rucksack over one shoulder,
which I hadn't noticed earlier.

The springs of Marla's bed creak
through the ceiling.

We can take booze to the shed, I suggest.
Lucy shrugs. I pour ample measures from
the decanter into tumblers
and
glug
glug
glug
to prove I am fun,
someone to invest in.

And in the shed,
as the world wheels around us
I giggle for no good reason,
and sing songs I've heard on the radio
but don't know the words to,
until Lucy opens her rucksack and

I spot Marla's clock from the mantelpiece—
a heavy heirloom she fondles most mornings.

As Lucy gets drunker,
laughter climbing
into the roof of the night,
I feel entirely empty
of everything.

Space

Marla stares at the   space
on the mantelpiece   but says

                     nothing.

Pointless

Lucy took the clock for no good reason
other than to have it
and for Marla not to have it
and to take it from a home
she thinks is mine
so I will not have it
or inherit it either.

Lucy stole the clock simply
to prove she could.

Lucy doesn't need stuff.
And she obviously doesn't need me.

Snickers Bar

Dad left a Snickers bar in the fridge door.
It was there weeks:
> cold,
> hard.

One day after school I took it,
ate it,
enjoyed every bit of it
with a Coke can
and Kelly-Anne's *People* magazine.

That night Dad said, *My Snickers is gone.*

Kelly-Anne looked up from her sudoku.
Not me. I'm too fat for any more chocolate.

I stared at my lap.
I took it, I muttered.

Dad didn't say any more,
just slammed the fridge door
and went to work
in a mood.

He always noticed when things went missing.

And sometimes he set me up.
    Taking the Snickers was exactly
    what he had wanted.
It gave him a reason for his rage.

The Blackbird

A blackbird is in the shed
while I am clearing
       away evidence of my evening with Lucy.

The bird blinks,
perched on rolled-up, rusting metal wiring.

I startle, scream,
but he doesn't move,
even when I come close.
       He blinks again.
       Fearlessly leers.

Is he injured or gutsy?
Did he see everything from last night?

I open the door   wide
so he can   fly free.

He turns away
and I'm too creeped out to
clean any more.

Back in the house,
Marla is watching TV with the sound down.

Stuff

How old is Marla now?
    Seventy-five perhaps.
    Eighty?
Will anyone want her things when she is gone?
    Who will get rid of them?

Marla's house does not contain surfaces.
Her walls are plastered with pictures and plates.
The shelves are stacked with books and
    knickknacks thick with dust.
    The candles are unlit,
        their wicks still white and waxy.

So many things,
    many she might miss
but which,
    at the end of the day,
mean very little
if anything
at all.

I hope.

Concern

The neighbor's dog
trapped himself in our yard
    and fastened his jaw to my face,
    chowed down.

The neighbor hit the poor hound with a shovel,
leaving me with only a punctured lip
and not a proper mauling,
though Kelly-Anne said
I looked like a bomb victim.

I wiped bloody hands
down my white T-shirt
and went inside.

Dad was watching from the window.
That'll stain if you don't bleach it, he said,
and went back to stirring soup.

Later he argued with our neighbor
over the wall
about unsafe pets
and compensation.

If I'd had the shovel,
    that dog wouldn't still be barking.

I didn't see the dog again:
    they had it put down.

A week later Dad bought a watch on eBay.

In Knots

Marla is trying to untie
the laces from a pair of
leather shoes in her lap.
Her fingers scratch the eyelets,
worry at tight knots.
She tuts and sighs constantly,
then shouts,
> *Jesus! Why can't I . . .*
> *Stupid fecking things!*
She flings the disobedient shoes
against the fireplace.
I pick them up, check the laces,
which are tight
but not impossible.
Don't! Marla is on the verge of tears.
Don't even try.

I wasn't going to, I lie,
seizing a pair of scissors
from her sewing basket
and snipping the laces away from the shoes.
We'll buy laces for them tomorrow.

She says,
Did we get the gig at the Tivoli?
I'll speak to Roger.
God, I hope he didn't give the job to Moira.
She's always sniffing around.
We'll practice tomorrow when we have shoes.
Are you free to dance tomorrow, Toff?

Yes, I tell her. *I am.*

What John Lennon Does

We dance.
Marla's choice of music.
The Beatles.
"Can't Buy Me Love."
Marla says,

> *Sure, will you smile, for Christ's sake.*
> *There's no use dancing if you're not going to mean it.*
> *There's no use having a high kick*
> *and fast twirl*
> *if you're going to look like a miserable mallard.*
> *Who pissed in your pond anyway?*

She gyrates and gestures,
closes her eyes,
and grins.

> *John Lennon always makes*
> *me cream myself.*

> *Marla!*

> *What? Well he does.*

After Donal

For only the second time since I've been with Marla,
Donal visits.
       The calendar says weekly,
but that's a lie.

He marches in—I hide.
His footsteps are heavy and possessive,
his voice a dark din.
       Peggy says she caught you dancing.
       And that's all great and everything
       until you have a fall
       and who'll have to deal with that?
       I got you a big TV so you'd have something to do.
       What more is it you need?

I'd like to see Mary.
Is she coming to visit soon?

       No, she isn't.
       Stop going on about it.

I wasn't. I just wondered.

Do you want me to change
the bulb in that lamp?

Yes, please.
You're very good, she says.

After he is gone,
> Marla dims
> like a candle
> blown out.

Are you still in there? I want to ask,
watching her eyes glaze over,
her mouth chewing on itself,
her hands busy with nothing.

Shall we dance? I try instead,
finding "Gangnam Style" on my phone,
playing it for her,
showing off the ridiculous moves,
searching for a pathway to her smile.

When does The Voice *start?* she asks.

I don't push her to be happy.
I go to the store for dinner,

leaving her alone to remember herself,
giving her time to creep out of

                the hole
                she is
                hiding in.

When she is ready
she will come back
and
I will be here.

Police

I set up the email on my phone,
log in to Facebook and Instagram.
Seconds later it is pinging and vibrating
like I'm the most popular person alive.

Dad has sent twelve angry emails,
mostly asking if I've blocked him on my phone,
twice threatening to call the police
     if I don't come home,
once telling me he is very sad alone.

Kelly-Anne emails too.
     Bude is a big place, Allison. Answer my calls.
     Or WhatsApp me. PLEASE.
     I'm waiting. And I'm worried.
     CALL ME, FFS.

The good thing about email is that no one
knows whether or not you've read the messages.
So I pretend I haven't.

I am not quite sure why I don't reply
to Kelly-Anne.
          I think Allison is gone.

I am Toffee now.

Loitering

A blackbird is perched on a branch
of the plum tree in the garden.
I saw him in the shed, I say.

The same one? Let's keep it as a pet.
I had a parrot once.
The cat ate it.
A cliché but not a lie.
Cat ate her own kittens too.
Horrible yoke.
Marla crosses her arms.
Why is he just sitting there? Is he sick?

I open the door.
The bird defiantly does not move.
Pain rims its yellowy eyes.
Are you sick? I say stupidly.
The blackbird opens its beak a bit,
taps it together—*click-clack*—but doesn't tweet.
Marla already has a saucer of water in her hands.
It's hurt, I say.
She goes to the bird,
holds out the dish.

Nothing stirs.

And then something does:
from beneath a bush
the gray cat I met on my first night in the shed,
    slinking with his
    tummy low,
    his eyes anchored to the blackbird.

The bird'll be grand, Marla says
for no good reason.
I'll get some seeds.
I think I have seeds.
Or we could get some grubs.
Daddy always has maggots for his fishing.
She searches for something in her memory,
then stares at the space around her like an answer
might be hidden in the air.
Where is Daddy?
Is Daddy at home?

We have seeds, I say, *and if we don't,*
I can go to the store to get some.
I help you now, not your daddy.
The cat edges along the garden.

You help me? Do I need help?

Sometimes.

And do I help you?
She peers at the motionless bird.

I shoo away the cat.
Yes. You help me all the time.

Small Talk

I muted the podcast when his car pulled up,
rubber squeaking against the path as he parked.

He saw me from the hall but didn't speak.

In the kitchen he sat at the table,
      rubbed the back of his neck with his hand.

I made pasta. I stirred a pot of penne,
      black olives in red sauce.
The meal was bland, I knew that,
but it was better than cereal
or frozen waffles cooked in the toaster.
Dad went to the window.

How was work?
It was a question regular people
asked each other—
      small talk about the day,
      a way of taking an interest.

I'd be better off on unemployment, he said,
picking at a blemish in the wooden table.
Give me some of that crap you've cooked.

He took out his phone and
aimlessly scrolled
through one app,
then another.

I dished the dinner into two bowls
                        and sat opposite him,
no longer hungry,
waiting for him to finish
so I could go to my room
and pretend to be busy.

The biggest crime on earth was laziness.

I didn't want him to catch me at it.

Wasted

I wasted a lot of time
waiting for my father to be a better person,
wondering if he could change,
        if *I* could change him
        by being quiet,
        disrupting his life
        as little as possible.

I should have used my time more wisely:
I could have counted the hairs on Sophie's dog;
I could have emptied a swimming pool
with a spoon;
I could have memorized Shakespeare's plays,
            the sonnets too.

I wasted precious time thinking
I could change my father

if only I were more
than I knew how to be.

Bra Shopping

I thought I'd done a good job hiding
my boobs behind layers
of vests and sweaters
but Kelly-Anne still noticed,
marched me down to the department store,
and made me choose some bras.

In the changing room,
half-naked, seeing myself full-length
for the first time,
I shouted back answers like:
 It's a bit tight. Too lacy. Too puffy!
while Kelly-Anne's hand kept creeping
under the door with new options.

Afterward we got Burger King.
Don't tell Dad about this, I said,
 not sure why he couldn't know.

Kelly-Anne stole a chicken nugget
   and bit into it.
I don't tell your dad anything, she said.
Her phone pinged and she laughed,

turned the screen around to me to show me
a video of a deer chasing a bear.

I knew then that everything was temporary,
that there was no way Kelly-Anne would stay.

Tweeting

A sound like optimism wakes me,
a bird with so much music in his tiny body
he is bullying us to begin the day—
    Wake up, come and see this world, he sings.
    Wake up, there are so many wonderful things.
    And here's me,
        a hundred times bigger
        with only half his voice
        and so little music
        inside me.

Could it be the brazen blackbird singing?
Could he have finally found his voice
    and come back to boast?

I look out the window.

A speckled sparrow is settled on the holly bush.

The blackbird is
nowhere
to be seen.

I get up and make pancakes.

Recycling

It is pouring rain,
white noise beyond the windows.

I slip my feet into Marla's rain boots,
clomp to the side of the house,
and pour a box of plastics
into the recycling bin.

By my feet a wet lump,
a clump of unflying feathers.

The blackbird is back,
this time with no nerve at all—
dead, still, soaking in the rain.

Water pummels me from the sky
but I won't let Marla find the bird.
      Wish I hadn't myself.
I pick him up,
      heavy in my bare hands,
and take him to the compost pile
at the back of the garden,
bury him in brown leaves.

I hope he will decay back into the earth
and return as something beautiful.

At the back door I hear a mewling.
A hungry cat on the hunt.

Scabby

Marla trips on the patio,
tears her tights,
bloodies her knee.

Within a week the cut
is a thick slab of scab
like knobbled rust.

She picks at its crusty edges,
risks ripping fresh flesh.

I push away her ferreting fingers.
Please stop.

We stare down at a loose flake.

One last bit, she begs.

And I do understand her need to pick,
finish the job,
the frustration of seeing something so frayed
and close to clean.

No.
I won't watch you hurt yourself.

Power

Butterflies loved my old bedroom.

In summer they wheeled in through open windows
         to dance
         before desperately seeking
         a way out.

There were days when I woke with
paper-thin wings on my face,
bands of butterflies
         tiptoeing in with
         the morning.

I tried to catch them,
tease them outside,
but they were so easily broken,
so easily crushed and killed.
I had to chase gently,
clasp my fingers together to
         trap them,
keep my hands a cave.

Before the release,
         I'd always hold the butterfly
         for a few extra seconds,

feel its flutter,
the fragile panic.

I could have crushed and killed it,
or gone outside and
      released it
      into the dandelions,
and knowing I had this power
always made me feel
a bit sick.

Beach Day

Marla roots under the stairs,
uncovers
        a pail and shovel
laced with spiderwebs.
She holds them aloft.
I can't dance all day long.
I've only one pair of knees.
I need to get out of the house.
So do you.

No way. It's a downpour, I say. *No way.*
Marla finds a raincoat and hands it to me.

I want to build something, she says.
I want to get dirt in my toenails.
I live near the beach, don't I?
I can smell the sailors.

I hesitate,
        watch her hopeful eyes,
        wonder whether or not to lie
        about how close we are to the sea.

        I mean, I could.
        I could easily lie.

Brief Encounter

The rain keeps the sand wet
        so we can build
        things that
        do not
        blow away with the wind.

We dig a hole,
line it with
towers,
        sharp battlements.

People watch us,
        the teenager and the old woman
        sitting in the sand,
        hands and hair dirty.

A little girl helps,
digging the hole deeper
so we can hide from pirates.
        I am a mermaid, she tells us.
        I am trapped on land. Help! Help!

Help! Marla repeats.
Help! I repeat.

Help. Help. Help.

The tide creeps toward us,
waves licking the edges of our fortress.

We have spent the afternoon building
but no one will remember
the work that went into it
or how bewitching it was—

how strong, solid.

Everything
eventually

will be washed away.

Captured

We wait and watch
until everything
has been flattened.

Until the sea has
captured the castle.

You Are Mine

I slip the key into the lock.
Marla says, *Where are we?*

Home, I say,
switching on the lights,
the white hallway
tinted green from the lampshade.

Marla blinks at me,
                              blank.

Toffee, I remind her.

I want someone else. Who do I want?
She traces a wonky line
in the wood–chip wallpaper
        with her fingernail.

You don't want me here? I ask.
I want to know the answer.

Tears pool in the corner of her eyes.
I do, she says.
But I want someone else too.

After the Summer Fair

When I introduced the goldfish to Kelly-Anne
she acted as though I'd adopted a baby.
Jesus Christ, Allie, are you crazy?

I need a bowl, I told her.
I was wearing face paint like a zebra.
I'd spent the day castle-bouncing
at my last summer fair before high school.

Kelly-Anne scattered chicken nuggets
      onto a baking tray and
      lobbed the whole thing into the oven.
A bowl and a new brain.
Have you even met your father?
She rummaged
under the sink
anyway
and found a dusty round vase.
Hide it, she warned.
And I know nothing about this.

Her name is Iris.
I kissed the side of Kelly-Anne's head.

She smelled like hair spray.
I was so glad she was my almost-mum.

Iris survived in our house
much longer than I expected.
        Years.

We all did, I suppose.

Iris

Get in here! Dad shouted
like I was some disobedient dog.

My skin started to tingle.
      What had I done wrong?
I wasn't late,
didn't leave him with an untidy house,
even made tuna sandwiches—
covered them in plastic wrap to keep the bread
    from drying out,
        the corners from curling.

I found him in the bathroom
holding the vase I used as a fishbowl
        over the toilet.
A vein in his neck throbbed.
And
        I knew what was coming.

Didn't we talk about pets? he asked.

I watched Iris swim in gulpy circles,
stupidly unaware her life was on the line.

I envied that about Iris:
she couldn't remember, or plan, or worry.
Some nights I watched her
        circling, circling, circling,
        deleting her memory as she swam,
        two fins up to the future.
I always wanted to be like that,
but my stubborn brain stockpiles everything—
the good, the bad, and the boring—
and when I'm alone
I scan,
        left and right,
looking at my life,
never able to find any safe place.

Whose house is this?

I bowed my head,
hoped that if I seemed sorry he'd settle down.
Yours, I said. *But—*

And what did I say when you asked for a cat?

He knew exactly what he'd said about a cat
because he doesn't have the memory
of a goldfish either.

He was making me suffer—
    forcing me to admit
        he was right,
        I was wrong.

I stepped into the bathroom.
I got her free at a summer fair
ages ago.
I didn't know what to do with her.

His lips twisted.
Yeah, what to do with a brainless goldfish?
        Here,
        let me show you.
Without a hint of hesitation he
        tipped the vase,
        poured the water
        and Iris
        into the toilet bowl, and
        flushed it.

So that was it.
Iris was gone,
drowned in piss and shit.

You'll listen next time, Dad said,
handing me the empty vase,
storming past Kelly-Anne
                        at the top of the stairs.

I didn't answer,
which was always the best way to deal with it.
And anyway, I knew it wasn't the last I'd hear of it.

My punishment had been too quick.

Birthday

                    I hide in my room,
Donal showing up unexpectedly,
suiting himself.

He murmurs a lot,
about Marla's unusual tidiness,
the cups in the right cupboards,
her hair, smooth instead of nesty.

Forget it, he says
over the noise of rugby.
You will anyway.

But I didn't know, Donal.
If I'd known I would have bought a card.
Maybe I did. Let me look.

Seriously, sit down.

I try to be a good mother.
Sometimes Mary hides things, I think.
She's here all the time hiding things.
Mary?

Can you zip it?

Am I a bad mother?
Donal, talk to me,
        I'm sorry.
I'm sorry.
Donal? Is Mary safe?
Or maybe I'm thinking of Louise.
Is Louise all right?

Louise is fine, Mum.
She's had a baby.

And she's my daughter.

No. Granddaughter.

And how is Mary?
How's my Mary?

Something bangs. A long silence.
Jesus, Mum, Mary's dead.
How many times do you want me to tell you?
It's been years. You have to stop.
I can't keep breaking the news like this.
Oh, don't cry.

He turns up the TV,

                      shuts her out.

I tiptoe into Marla's room,
take the cellophane-wrapped card
from her dressing table,
drop it
into the
wastebasket.

The calendar pinged a reminder last week.
I bought the card from the drug store,
        golf clubs on the front,
        Happy Birthday, Son.

But he isn't getting it.
Donal isn't getting any Happy Birthday.

Soothing

She can hardly breathe,
choking on sobs.
A child's birth, forgotten.
A child's death, gone too.
Who am I?
Who am I?

I stroke her hand.
You're still a mother.
You're still Marla.
That stuff doesn't change.

Everything has changed.
I just can't remember.

I hold her in my arms.
        Her body shudders.
And by the time she has cried herself to sleep
she has forgotten what her tears
were about in the first place.

So Maybe

I try to make Marla believe she is a good mother,
      was,
but I've got no way of knowing how she
treated Donal and Mary thirty years ago
or why Donal seems so angry.
I trust she was gentle and fun,
      the Marla now living.

And if she wasn't, maybe that's okay too—
maybe fewer memories means
she can be kinder,
         forgetting what made her bad.
      Unlike most of us
she lives in each day,
      not stuck in dreaming or worry.

So maybe Dad could mellow
if he got ill like her,
remembering only the good stuff
we had,
      the times I made him happy,
and forgetting all the ugly details of our past,
his past,
the reasons for his rage.

Still My Mother

I don't care that I have no pictures
of me and Mum together.

And I don't have memories either.

Because I lived in her body for nine months
and knew her from the inside.
She loved me.
I know she did.

I feel it in my gut.

And nothing will ever stop me
from loving her back.

How Worried?

I reread Dad's last email, his last line.
    Call me, okay? I'm worried.

But how worried can he really be
about me
when he hasn't found me?

There are ways to do these things.
It isn't easy to disappear.

It isn't just diseases that make people
forget their kids.

Breakfast

Marla stirs a bowl of muesli,
tastes it, spits.
That's pure sawdust.
I'm not eating that.
Have we any cake?
I could murder some angel food.
I'll ask Mary to pick one
up on her way over.

It's not supposed to be dry, I tell her.
I do not remind her Mary will
never visit again.
       What would be the point
       in making her relive that pain?

She reaches for the carton of apple juice
         and pours.

I wait for the reaction
       and, when it is a sneaking smile,
leave her to enjoy her cereal.

Imbalance

Dark.
Night.
A knock so sharp I shudder,
should ignore it.

Don't.

Why?

Why can't I
go upstairs
and keep the world in balance?

A knock so sharp I shudder.
Night. Moonlight.
Owls hoot. Darkness.

Why?

Why don't I say no?

Why can't I ever just
say
no.

What I Don't Know

Open up.
Lucy presses her tongue to the kitchen window.
I can't smell her,
but I know she's drunk,
stupid,
dangerous.

What I don't know until it's
             too late,
             until I've
                    opened the back door,

is that
she has company.

A Consolation

You can't be here.
You can't be here.
You have to go.
You have to go now
before she wakes up.
Lucy. Stop. Lucy.
You can't be here.

They are foraging in the fridge,
drinking milk straight from the bottle,
biting into blocks of cheese,
> laughing,
> comfortable,
> nothing not theirs.

You already know Jan and Mindy.
That's Kenny and Joel. He's Mark.

I tear Marla's tea cozy from a boy's head.
Go home.
Lucy, she'll be so confused if she wakes up.
Please. Please.

Lucy stands soldier straight,
        salutes.
Right, troops. Be cool.
Don't act like savages.
And to me:
        We'll be good. I promise.
A kiss to the tip of my nose.

They are quieter.
Sneaking.
But they are not good.

They move to the sitting room,
lie on her sofa,
loll on her chairs,
poke fun at her photos.
They help themselves to booze,
splosh it on her carpet.
They find trinkets and pocket them.
Put that back.
That isn't yours.
But behind me I know something else
is being taken,
perhaps something that means more.

Upstairs nothing stirs.

Marla sleeps.
She dreams through it all.

And it is a consolation.

Assault

In the low lamplight
I straighten the room,
rearranging cushions,
wiping down the coffee table.
But in the bathroom
I can't do much about
the piss-soaked bath mat.
        I take it out to the
trash.
On the patio
one of Marla's
porcelain dolls lies
naked,
her head
        cracked open
against the
concrete.

In the Daylight

Marla finds a pair of earbuds
in the pocket of her cardigan.
She struggles to understand.
But then again,
                    so do I.

Bad Weather

Marla is back in bed,
her head beneath the covers.
I peel back a corner of the duvet,
                              find her face.
Are you asleep? I whisper.

No.

Are you hungry? I ask.

I don't know.
I want to stay here.
Peggy said I could stay here
until the clouds have gone.
It feels very cloudy today.

I pull the duvet back further,
climb into the bed next to her,
both of us fully dressed.
It's really cloudy for me too.
We can get up later, I say.
I press my forehead against her shoulder,
feeling my way through the fog.

Who Did That to Your Face?

She asks.

My Dad Did It

I tell her.

Sulking

Kelly-Anne had been gone a month.
Dad rarely alluded to her,
went on about other things instead—
    the state of the house,
    traffic—
as though these were real reasons
to be awful.

I kept out of his way.
    A hurricane was coming.
    The air stank of a storm.

I used a little jug to fill the iron with more water;
steam sizzled through the holes in the hot plate.
    It was a Sunday evening.
    I was just sorting out my school uniform.

Where's my wallet? Dad grunted,
    appearing out of nowhere,
    breathing heavily.

I haven't seen it, I said
without looking up.
I didn't want to instigate anything.
    Plus,
    I'd started to hate him.

You're sulking
like you did that time
about the fish, he said.

I kept my back straight—eyes on my school skirt.
How are storms defeated except by
hunkering down defensively?
I don't know what you mean.

He rested his fists on the ironing board.
Look at me when we're speaking.

Sorry, Dad, I said quickly,
              remembering myself.

You heard from Kelly-Anne? he asked.

Well.
I heard from Kelly-Anne a lot,
knew she was living by the sea.
Happy.
              No.

He closed one eye, peered at me with the other.
I've heard from Kelly-Anne myself.

I inched away.
The iron hissed.

She told me she's spoken to you lots.
Full of secrets aren't you?
So what else are you hiding?
What else is there?
His voice was calm,

                serene before
        the savage.

Your wallet, I said, spotting it and
snatching it from the empty fruit bowl behind him.
I turned to reveal his treasure,
but he didn't care,
he had the iron
in his hand,
and
he was
swinging,

             swinging,

                          swinging,

putting all his
weight behind him,
his face fire.

Get Up

I was a ball on the floor by the fridge,
shivering and shuddering
and wondering if it was all over
or if he had more fight in him.

It was navy dark outside
but the Sullivans were still in their yard,
drinking beers and playing backgammon,
making neighborly noises.
I thought:
   Why can't my life be a bit more that,
   a bit less this?
   Less of him.

The Sullivans squealed.
Their new puppy yapped like it was being teased.
Delighted squeals.
Happy yapping.

My face throbbed—
a red-hot pain too tender to touch,
bruised and swollen.

I lay on the linoleum
shaking,

aching,
watching his feet near my face
pace
       up and down.

You aren't hurt. Get up, he said.

But my body was a brick—
heavy and crumbling at the corners.

Get up, he said again,
and I wanted to,
staring at the dust and dried-up pasta
underneath the oven.
                    All that hidden dirt.

I wanted to say, *Help,*
       but didn't.
I wanted to get up.

Before I got the chance he was
toeing my tummy with his sneaker.
       Are you okay, Allie? he said,
sounding surprised,

like he thought I was made of metal,
like he didn't hear me whinny,
see
me
fall.

He sighed finally. *I'm going to be late.*
Clean up before you go to bed.

I tried to blink away the burning.
I tried to push away the pain.

It didn't work. I couldn't.

Understanding

We are still beneath the duvet.
Marla holds my hand.
You didn't deserve that.

Thing Is

A big part of me believes I did deserve it,
        every bit,
and all the years before it too.

I wasn't, wasn't, wasn't.

If it was about someone else,
why didn't he stop?

Acceptance

Marla lets go of my hand.
None of it was ever about you.
It was about him.
It's always all about them.
Surely you know that?

Different Lessons

When teachers gave me problems to solve,
numbers to conquer,
shapes to calculate,
no matter how hard they were,
I always figured out the answers
with time and a pencil.

Mrs. Sanders said,
You aren't a genius, Allison Daniels,
but you're smart enough.

What use is smarts now?

She said,
Keep it up
and you'll go places, young lady.

But she never imagined my life.
She didn't know I needed
different lessons.

Advent

They turn on the Christmas lights
along the main street.
The promenade glitters
with bright white snowflakes.
I have looked at dancing shoes
for Marla.
I have spent two pounds
on mince pies.

I need a tree, she tells Donal excitedly.
Waste of money, he replies.

　　She doesn't argue.
　　It is decided.

Hamless

Last Christmas . . . was it last year?
It was after Mam died.
Was it Mam who died?
> She spots something in the distance,
> shakes herself back.
Daddy made the dinner.
But didn't he forget to cook the ham?
He sent us all out to mass
and afterward we went down to Granny's
to give her the scarf Niamh had knitted.
Niamh's great at knitting.
A bit addicted. A bit boasty.
Good at everything.
Butter wouldn't melt.
> *She's got grandchildren now.*
> *Granny loved the scarf.*
The priest looked hungover.
Too many baby Jesus beers the night before,
> *if you know what I mean.*
We got home half-starved.
I set the table.
I couldn't smell meat.

Niamh helped Daddy dish it all out.
    "Daddy," she says.
    "Where's the ham?" she says.
And holy Santy balls, that was it.
She might as well have called him
a heathen.
Back of the hand, she got.
Upstairs she was sent.
So it was just me and Daddy at the table
in these gold paper hats,
eating fecking carrots and rock-hard spuds
for Christmas.
He was a gobshite after Mam went.
She left him.
No, she died.
She left us all.
He hit her too. He shouted. Still does.
Shall we go to the movies?
We could ask Roger for an advance on the money.
Do you have any money?
We could ask Mary maybe.

    I kiss her cheek.
    I'll get our coats, I say.
    Let's go out.

The Beach

Seagulls swoop, owning the sky.
Each one has their own war cry
and can identify another's tune.

Would anyone know my voice
if they heard it ring out?

In my pocket, my phone pings.

Please

Another email from Kelly-Anne.
    I'm traveling to Cornwall
    tmrw in case you're down there.
    Please tell me you're safe.
    CALL ME. I've tried a hundred times.
    KA xxxx

I do not reply.
I do not know what to say
anymore to anyone
I used to know.

Grease

I was an extra in the school production of *Grease*.
Sophie got the part of Sandy
and had to wear stupid tight trousers
and platform shoes in the last scene.
Not really a feminist statement, Sophie, Jacq said to her.
Changing your appearance for a guy and whatever.

Sophie ran her hand over her ass.
I look good though. Admit.

Dad and Kelly-Anne
came to watch the final performance.
They sat at the back,
Dad with his face in his phone.

Afterward he said, *Your pal was good.*
Pair of lungs on her.

She's in the choir, I explained.

Kelly-Anne put an arm around my shoulder.
You were excellent, Allison.

Dad was laughing.
Choir?
It's a long way from church where she'll end up.
  I predict that with complete certainty.

On the walk home we stopped for snacks,
Dad letting me choose between an ice pop
or a bag of Doritos,
   but not both.
Well done with your singing, he said,
handing the cashier a five.
I almost managed a smile
until he added,
  You did your bit admirably.
  Not everyone is born to be a star.

I Am Allison

Watching the news,
politicians peddling lies
dressed up to look like promises,
Marla turns.
Who are you? she asks sadly.

I'm Allison.
I'm here because I've got nowhere else to go.

Oh. Marla nods.
I've nowhere else to go either.

The Sea

The sea does not care
whether I am smiling in silk
or sobbing in torn skirts.

The sea
will come in
        and out
will breathe
        and rage
and settle
        despite everything
I am shouting
at the shoreline.

The sea listens only to its own voice
and not the noise of those who'd tell it
how to behave.

I wish I could be more like the sea.

Fallen

I stop.
Watch a girl skateboarding down some steps.
I dawdle.
Missing the lights at a crosswalk.
I examine an ad in the newsstand
for a paper-delivery person.

I don't want jobs from Lucy anymore.

I walk slowly,
and by the time I am home
Marla is mewling,
crumpled at the bottom of the stairs,
a red blood-pillow beneath her head.

This Time

I cannot stop the blood.
I've got no choice.
I have to phone for help.

Paramedics

Marla is alive,
      stretchered into an ambulance
by paramedics
who assume I'm her granddaughter.
      You can sit there, they say,
      and I am by her side.
A plastic mask obscures her face;
the blanket is up to her chin.

Her eyes are on me.
Toffee.
I missed you.
Where have you been?
I needed someone to talk to about Mary.
You're the only one who would've understood.
Did you ever get over little Oliver?
Will I be okay ever again?

You fell.
You'll be fine.

Oh, yes. I did.
But see . . .
      I have been falling for a long time.

Passing On

You're family? the doctor asks.

　　Yes.

Well, she took a bad fall.
I'd say she blanked. She can't remember.
We'll keep her here awhile
but she'll have to find somewhere
with no stairs, I'd say.
　　　At the very least.
Can I leave this to you to pass on?

　　Yes. I'll tell her son.
　　My father.
　　Her son.

He frowns. *Right. Well. Good night.*

Mine

I leave a fake note from the paramedic
explaining to Peggy what's happened.
I hear her downstairs.

Shit. Shit. Shit. Shit.

And on the phone.

A fall . . . Yes . . . I don't know . . .
I'll go to the hospital now.

Then on the phone again:

A fall . . . Yes . . . I don't know.
I spoke to Donal.
Yes, he will.
I will.
Okay, Louise.
Yes.

She leaves.
She does not come back.

The house is mine.

Keeping Busy

With nothing better to do, I clean:
dishes, cupboards, floors.
I mop, wipe, polish, rub, buff,
and ignore the silence coming from

every place
        where Marla

       used to be.

Asleep

Her head is wrapped in clean white bandages.
Her skin is like paper.
Beside her a machine outlines her heartbeat—
                    alive,
          alive,   still alive.
I sit by her bedside.
She doesn't wake up.
I'll have to go away, I say.
I can't stay in the house when you're not there.
It wouldn't be okay.
Marla?

Behind me a nurse is checking
another patient's chart, tutting.

Marla moans in her sleep.

What?

Stay, she says.

Here or at the house? I ask.

Stay, she repeats.

And that is when Peggy appears by the bed too.

Peggy Appears by the Bed Too

Who are you?
Her thick hands are on her thick hips,
her thick lips are unsmiling, suspicious.

I stand and reach out a hand.
        I'm Allison, I tell her.
        I'm Marla's friend.
        I live down her street.

The Call

I've only had Messenger
installed a few hours when the call
     comes through,
and the voice I fear is there.
Where are you, Allison?

I stare at my screen.
Why did I answer?
What was I thinking?
He has found me.
He has found me
and will make me suffer now.
I've been asking everywhere, he says.
I was so worried.
Allison? Allison, answer me.
Is Kelly-Anne with you?

I'm not coming home, I say.
I'm safe.

Beyond the window, a car revs its engine.
A girl shouts.
A man laughs.
Somewhere a lawn mower is grinding grass.

So you did run away. There I was thinking
you'd been murdered and dumped in a ditch.
I've been a wreck, Allison.

A pause.

You hurt me.
You hurt me, Dad.
And not just that last time.
All the time.

The words are spoken out loud.
      Not a murmur in my head.
      Not a question.
      Not an apology.
The words are spoken out loud.

You didn't have to run away.
We could have talked.
Did Kelly-Anne put you up to it?
And you hurt me too, you know.
He coughs into the mouthpiece.
Did she already have the baby?
She wouldn't even give me the chance to be sorry.
One mistake. One mistake.

The room buzzes,
all the electricity running through the walls
suddenly screeching.
She was pregnant?

She stole one kid and made the other one hate me.

Of course.
Yes.
Pregnant.
Of course.

I shut off the phone,
drop to the carpet,
curl up,
and cry harder
than I
ever have before.

No Answer

Kelly-Anne doesn't reply to
any of my messages.
She isn't even reading them
and I haven't got her number
to call
      so I send her my new one.
PLEASE CALL ME ASAP.
I'M SO SORRY. A xxxxx

I check every three minutes
for some sign she's seen me.

Where is she?
Where is she?
Where is she?

The Fire

The point of a lit match
against a fire starter
        that squeaks and burns up like Styrofoam,
the flame catching hold of
newspaper fists
beneath a scaffolding of twigs and logs.

The fire crackles, pops, smokes
through the empty room.

On the rug,
I stare into the flitting flames,
my scar coming awake with the heat.

I stoke the blaze,
jabbing with a heavy poker,
forcing the white ash from the log edges to fall
                                        away,
aiming for an inferno,
something to drink me up.

I have never been so alone.

Intruder

I awake to smolder, cinders,
the fire cooling in the grate,
and to a clatter in the hallway.

I stay still,
curl myself into a ball
like I might
blend in with the paisley-patterned rug.

There is muttering
and someone ascending the stairs.

      A light.

Quickly
      I crawl
         behind the sofa,
try not to breathe.
A rattling around;
      drawers in Marla's room opened,
      slammed shut,
      wardrobes raided.

You need to come here, Donal snaps,
and at first I think he might be summoning me,
but he goes on.
I'm rooting through her knicker drawer.
I don't want to see my mum's knickers.
You've gotta come here.
Or she's gotta go to you.
She needs a woman.
She can't take care of herself
and I haven't time for it, Louise.
If Mary was alive I'd ask her
but she isn't.
I don't want to burden you, I just . . .

He's on the phone.
Collecting things for the hospital.
Donal's here doing what I could have done
if I hadn't been so thoughtless,
squandering time feeling sorry for myself
instead of being helpful.

Yeah, well, I'm at the end of my rope
and I've been saying for a long time
that she doesn't need this house.
Something has to give.

He searches awhile longer,
clanging, banging,
no attempt to treat Marla's home gently,
and then he is gone,
not bothering to give the house
a once-over,
but warning me nevertheless
that my time here is
                    running
                        out.

Packing

I leave behind anything Marla gave me—
    socks and slippers,
    books and pens—
    in a pile on the end of the bed.

It isn't right for me to live here now.

And anyway,

I have to find somewhere
before someone finds me.

I wish Kelly-Anne would find me.

Free-Falling

I am not suicidal
but up on this cliff top,
      the wind heavy-breathing against my neck,
the foamy waves jeering,
I imagine how easy
              a slip would be,
how I could find a few seconds of relief in
free-falling
and then
                    nothing.

I am not suicidal
but there are days when I do not
want to
be.

The hanging on.

It is so hard.

Jazz

Marla is watching the ceiling fan turn,
a cannula in her arm.
Hey, I say.
She sits up straighter. Smiles.
I brought you this.
It is a box wrapped in red paper,
cheap ribbon around it.

She rips at the wrapping,
opens the lid, and yelps.
Jazz shoes!
In pink?
Jazz shoes in pink!
She holds one to her chest,
      kisses the toe
        like you might the nose of a new puppy.

They're for Christmas.
It's Christmas tomorrow.
I sit on her bed,
place one hand on her leg.

Why won't I see you on Christmas? she asks.
We can have visitors whenever we like.

I force my finger into a hole in the blanket.
Marla puts the shoes back into the box,
passes it all to me, and says,

> Take those home and hide them from Donal.
> When I get out of here
> we'll get going on a routine.
> I won't have anyone beating us to it.

She presses her mouth to my ear.

> That's the best present I've ever had in my life,
> and when I was gorgeous,
> fellas bought me diamonds.
> I had a boyfriend who died.
> He was a right old codger—too old for me.
> Sure didn't he leave me his boat?
> I couldn't keep it.
> Told the lawyer to give it to his son
> and then didn't I find out he had a wife.
> A wife!
> So she got the bloody boat.
> Dirty old bastard.
> How did you know I liked to dance?

I chew on my thumb knuckle.

> *Allison?* she says.
> *How did you know?*

I Am Allison

I am Allison.
I am Allison.
I am Allison.
And the world still spins.

She Will Know

I
buy
a tree
so that when
Marla comes home
she will smile and know it is
Christmas. I buy a tall tree and cover it in
ornaments and colored lights. For when Marla comes
HOME.

The Other Side

I watch *Mary Poppins*,
eat frozen pizza,
and listen to the sounds
of Christmas coming from outside—
      carols through car radios,
      families drunk and happy by noon.

And
           when it's afternoon visiting hours,
I go to the hospital,
where Marla is wearing a party hat
and watching the Queen's Christmas Message.
Lizzy got very old, she says.
And she needs a decent bra.
With all the money
you'd think someone would find her
a bit of support.

A nurse smiles.

Peggy saunters in.
It's you again.
Don't you have a home to go to?

No, I admit.

Peggy shrugs, hands Marla a gift.
Would someone turn that claptrap off?
Bake Off *is on the other channel.*

Boxing Day

His energy is in the elevator.
I can feel it on my way up.
And there he is by her bedside,
berating her.

> *Do you have to make that*
> *noise through your mouth?*

I interrupt.
Do you mean her breathing?
Would you like her to stop?
I laugh. It is fake.
Donal does a double take,
lifts his chin.
He has fluff in his beard.
Hey, Marla!
I got you a bag of Twizzlers.
They'll rot your dentures.

Who are you? Donal demands.

Me? I'm Allison.
And I know all about you, Donal.
Lovely to meet you.
I do not think he can tell I am a teenager.

Perhaps my tone
suggests social worker.

He stands. Downs something
from a polystyrene cup.
Time is up on my parking meter.
I'll be back in a few days, he says.
See you later, Mum.

Marla watches him walk away.

Your son, I remind her,
is a bit of a bastard.

Kelly-Anne Calls

And all I can do is cry.
It's okay, she says over and over.
It's okay,
it's okay,
it's okay.

Is it?

The Sun-Up Bakery

Kelly-Anne pulls apart an almond croissant,
hands me one half
    though I've got a muffin of my own—
    blueberries oozing from its crusty lid.
So, she says.
Yeah, I say.
I'm sorry, she says.
I'm *sorry*, I say.
He's the one who should be sorry, she says,
pushing my hair back from my face.
Did he do that? Did he?
Pastry drifts into my lap.
    Kelly-Anne gently brushes the crumbs away
    from my skirt.
    Her fingers are swollen.
Where are you living? she asks.
I'm fine, I say.
I was worried, she says. *I came to find you.*
I almost went back to London.

He'd have killed you, I say.
I don't know whether or not
I'm being dramatic.
I might mean it.

When are you due?
        I finally glance at her belly.

Next week.
        I'm terrified.
Do you know how big a baby's head is?

I lay my hand on her bump.
The baby swims around
        inside her like a
        jellyfish,
turning the surface of her tummy
into moving mounds.

How did it get there? I find myself saying.
Kelly-Anne grins,
doesn't understand the question.

But I am thinking of my father.
How did something as beautiful as a baby
happen without anyone getting hurt?

You only took off once your *kid was at risk*, I say.
I am trying to explain how she let me down.

She touches my chin. *I have a place. Come with me.*

Apartment

Kelly-Anne's studio is smaller
than Marla's sitting room.
The kitchen is a sink,
microwave on the countertop,
a shelf above
with one mug, one glass, a plate.
It smells of nail polish.
Don't say it's nice.
I know it's awful.
She winces,
                    grips her tummy.

You can't stay here, I say.
I have somewhere we can go.
Not forever.
But for tonight.

In Marla's House

It would do no good
to tell Kelly-Anne the whole
truth
      and nothing but the truth,
so
instead
I make her tea and
change the bedsheets
and vaguely mention Marla's
hospitalization from a fall and not
from her confusion.
She isn't a weirdo, is she? Kelly-Anne wonders.

Unlike Lucy,
Kelly-Anne avoids touching things,
won't lean against the walls
for the first hour.
You sure she wouldn't mind me staying?

I say no because it's the truth.
I don't think Marla would mind.

Even so.
I keep the lights low and the curtains drawn.

Always

Marla is sitting up in her hospital bed.
Kelly-Anne shakes her hand
hello
     and when I see in Marla's eyes
that she has forgotten me
I shake her hand too
and say,
        Did they hard-boil your egg again?

Hard-boil it?
They baked and varnished it.

Probably 'cause of salmonella.
Kelly-Anne smiles.

They're just trying to needle me.
I overheard a nurse saying I was tricky.
Anyone would think I was a magician.
Tricky?
They wouldn't know what to do if
I got difficult.
Is that a baby you have in there
or did you have a big feed for breakfast yourself?

Kelly-Anne doesn't seem to hear.
She leans back into the chair suddenly and
whistles, her eyes wide.
She breathes hard through clenched teeth.

No, I say. No, not now, please.

Now isn't that tidy?
If we were in a film you'd roll your eyes.
Marla presses the Call button.
Make sure they give you plenty of drugs.
Don't be a hero.

Kelly-Anne starts to cry.
I'm so alone, she says.

We all are, I say.
But now we're alone together.

Demi-Sister

When I hold Helena's kitten-body
     close,
feel her saw-toothed spine
against my arm,
I can't remember how I ever
lived without her.

Louise

Peggy is talking quickly
while Marla looks at the wall.
Here's your pal.
Peggy scoots her chair sideways
       to make room for me.
I was just talking to Marla about how exciting
it'll be to move to Portsmouth.
Louise is down there.
Peggy lowers her voice.
She's Mary's girl.
I don't know whether you knew she had children.

I've come across Donal.

Marla pulls at the IV line.
I told you already. I like my house.
I need new carpet on the stairs,
that's all.

Peggy leans in.
It isn't immediate.
We'll get you packed up
and take all your things down there with you.

Marla reaches for me.
Her eyes are sad.
I only just got you back
and now we have to say goodbye again.
I can't say goodbye again, Toffee.

Forever

No goodbye is forever
unless you can
erase everything you ever
knew about a person and
everything you once felt.

I left Dad a few months ago
and decided
      that was it—
I was drawing a line under
knowing him.
But sometimes I wake with his voice in my ears
and his maybe-love in my guts
and I remember everything good about
him that has been left behind
and forget the bad,
and it makes me so sad
I wish I had the courage to call him
and beg for him to be better.

Mum has been dead my whole life
and not a day goes by when I don't think
about how we would have been together—

all the spaces left empty where
she should have stood.

No goodbye is forever
unless you can
erase everything you ever
knew about a person and
everything you once felt.

Marla Is Home

Kelly-Anne came back with Helena
and made them a nest in the room that was mine.
I have to confess something, I told her a few days later.

She threw a rattle at me
when I explained
what was what.
      We're squatters! she shouted.

We hide in the shed
the day Marla comes home,
the three of us like fugitives,
until we are sure Peggy and Donal have gone
and Marla is alone again.

Blank

The line of daylight drops down out of sight.
I take Kelly-Anne and Helena in the back door.
Marla is playing Scrabble with herself,
      tiles of letters littering the table.
Is ramrod a word? she asks.

Kelly-Anne snickers.
Helena wails.

Marla straightens up.
I don't know why you're so pleased.
Have you seen yourself?

Kelly-Anne's shirt is patchwork baby barf.
Her hair is wild, eyes sunken.

Give that child here to me.
Marla's arms make Helena helplessly limp.
You need a rest, young one, Marla says.
She is looking at Kelly-Anne.
Go on up and have a lie-down.
We'll call you down for Hollywood Squares.

In and Out

Did you put up the tree? Marla asks.

You noticed.

Ah, now.
I'm not gone totally King George bonkers just yet.
Is that what you think?
That I don't know a thing at all?
If I had the knees for it I'd get up and
give you a smack.

You come in and out of yourself, I say.

She laughs.
Sure, don't we all?

You Owe Me

The sand is wet, hard,
easy to stroll along without sinking.
Marla walks on ahead with Kelly-Anne.
I rock the stroller.

And then Lucy is there,
a girl next to her
with close-cropped hair like brown moss.
Before I can hide, she has seen me,
  grimaces like I am something rotten,

        and walks my way.

You owe me work.
She is focusing on my scar.
Behind her the girl is on the phone.

Oh, right, I say,
ready to collapse into myself.
And then a new voice comes out of nowhere.
You owe me money, I say.
You owe me eight quid.

Lucy hesitates. *I don't think I do.*

You do.

Look, I . . .

Give me what I'm owed.

It's just eight quid.

I make my face a rock.
A seagull circles overhead.

Lucy reaches into her bag and pulls out a wallet.
I only have a ten.

I'll take that.
I grab the money.

In the stroller Helena is grimacing
like she might be filling her diaper.
Appropriately.

Doughnuts

With the ten
we buy bags of hot doughnuts
and eat them competitively—
      trying not to lick the sugar
      from our lips
      until we've finished.

Marla wins by wolfing
down a doughnut
in two bites.

Where's my medal? she says.

Calling Dad

His voice is sandpapery tired
when I call to tell him

all the things
he did to sink me,

and by the end of the conversation
he is unconvinced,
unchanged,
angry.

But I am not.

In Need

The morning is spent watching Helena,
so Kelly-Anne can fix up the apartment
with fresh paint and bright curtains.
She insists she will have space for all of us.

Even so,
        I go to the housing authority
and make my case
as someone in need.

I'm not sure what will happen to my father now.

Enrollment

The students crash into one another,
laughing, swearing, tipping trays,
while teachers pretend not to notice,
hunched over their lunches like crows.

The school smells of pudding and bleach.

The principal enrolls me immediately.
Starting next week then, she says brusquely,
ushering a nosebleeding boy
into her room with an eye roll.
Fighting again, Philip?
For the love of . . .

I count on my fingers the weeks left
until my exams.
Kelly-Anne says, *Will you survive this place?*
It's a zoo.

I laugh.
You know this is how every public school
in the country feels?

She grimaces.
I'm glad I'm not sixteen.

A bell rings loudly and
the corridor is quiet.
The noise is just noise, I say.
I'll survive it.

What Happened to Toffee?

Marla smells of cookies.
The bright light outside has faded to salmon.
What happened to Toffee? I ask.
Marla's breathing is heavy.
Maybe she's asleep.
Part of me hopes she is, so that my question
can get lost in the evening.

Toffee? You don't sound a bit like yourself.
Are you coming down with something?
If you're well enough later will we go for a picnic?
We can take some jam sandwiches and crisps.
                Is it warm enough for picnics?
We can wear our coats.
She has a run in the foot of her tights.
Her toes caress the carpet.

Was she happy in the end? I ask.

Happily ever after?

Yes.

        Exactly.
        Can I have one of those?

Can Toffee be the kind of girl
who got the good stuff,
who didn't spend her whole life wishing.

Marla puts her hand on my knee.
Toffee was always braver than I was.
I mean, I pretended to be brave.
I talked a load of old bollocks and wore bright colors.
I flirted with boys much older
and I did things that made Daddy's hair curl.
Toffee didn't.
No. She was dead serious.
She wore brown even in the summer.
Sensible. You know what I mean?
And then she left. I stayed.
But she left. Not just for England,
wasn't a soul in the street who didn't go to England.

She ran away? I ask.

No. Marla sits up.
She left after Oliver died.
She took a boat and a suitcase to Brooklyn.
Did she survive the trip?
I don't know.
I don't know.

She never wrote from where she went.
She should have written at least.
Why didn't you write?
A stamp wouldn't have broken the bank.
She turns to me and I'm forced to see she is crying.
But you came back. Didn't you?
Everything works out in the end.
You're okay.
I'm okay.
The tears are on her chin.
She wipes them away with the back of her fingers.
I have to leave, don't I?

Yes, I say. *But it will all be okay.*
I think it really might be okay.

Final Act

Kelly-Anne is clapping.
Helena is dribbling.
Marla and I are puffing and panting
as we go through the old routine again,
for an audience this time:

right foot forward,
       right foot back,
right foot
right foot
right foot
right.
Left foot now,
forward and back,
left foot
left foot
left foot
left.

Collapsing on half-packed cardboard boxes,
Marla and I laugh
so hard my whole face is sore.

But it is no longer burning.

Leaving

Oh, it's you.
Peggy closes the trunk.

Marla is standing at the gate in
a long red coat,
her handbag over one shoulder.
Toffee.
　　　She
　　　　　　　　　reaches out.
I'm going somewhere.
A small child whooshes by on a scooter.
A frantic mother scrambles to keep up.
Are you coming too?

I take her hand.
It is thin, dry, warm.
I've signed up for dance classes, I say.
It is the truth:
at the Methodist Church on a Saturday morning,
swing and salsa—
All Ages Welcome.

Right, let's hit the road, Peggy sings.

I think I'm going somewhere, Marla repeats.

I borrowed a book from you.
I haven't finished it, I say.
It's called Moon Tiger.
I couldn't turn the last page when I tried.
Can I keep it?

She turns to face me.
Her eyes are pleading,
and then
        her arms are around my neck
and the rough wool from her coat
is against my cheek.
I miss you, she says.
I miss you and you're right here.

I hold on for as long as I can.
And when I let go
and look at her
I know
it's unlikely we will meet again,
and if we do
she won't recognize me.

But still.

In some secluded corner of our minds
we will both always remember.

And hopefully we can forget too.

Taillights

A hand waving from the passenger window.
Taillights gleaming against the gray day.
It will rain by noon.
And then it will be fine again.

It will.